SHARK

PINE RIDGE
BOOK THREE

ASHLEY A. QUINN

TCA PUBLISHING

Copyright © 2022 by Ashley A Quinn

This book is a work of fiction. The names, characters, events, and places are either products of the writer's imagination or have been used fictitiously and are not to be construed as real. Any resemblance to persons, living or dead, actual events, locales, or organizations is entirely coincidental.

No parts of this book may be copied, reproduced, and/or distributed in any way without express written consent from the author.

ISBN is 9798985344141
Library of Congress Control Number: 2022904853

One

Music blasted through Sara Katsaros's bluetooth speaker, filling the kitchen. She hummed along as she prepped meatloaf for tomorrow. Once she was done with these, she planned to make more pie crust and freeze it, so she had it for later this week.

Banging sounded over the music. Sara paused, wrist deep in meatloaf mixture. She glanced at her hands, then to the back door. "Dammit." She shook her hands, trying to remove some of the meat and egg coating her fingers.

Sighing, she grabbed a handful of paper towels, wiping them the best she could as whoever was on the other side banged on the metal door again.

"I'm coming, I'm coming," she grumbled. Tossing the towels in the trash, she grabbed a few more, so she didn't have to touch the handle with her yucky fingers.

The door rattled again as she reached it. With a huff, she unlocked it and twisted the knob, throwing it open. "What? Oh. Marci. Hi. What are you doing here?" She frowned as she saw her friend, Marci Red Feather standing on the other side, glaring at her. "Is something wrong?"

"Damn straight, something's wrong. Did you forget what tonight is?"

A frown marred Sara's brow for a split second before she groaned and looked skyward. "I'm sorry. I totally forgot." She and Marci were supposed to be at the Stone Creek for a girls' night so Daisy could tell them all about her honeymoon.

"You sure did, sunshine. Which is the reason Daisy and I are your only friends. We're the only ones who love you enough to put up with your one-track mind."

Sara blew her bangs off her face as she sighed. She wasn't wrong there. If they hadn't moved away, her old friends eventually just stopped calling because she didn't have time for them. Marci was the only one who really stuck by her. And now there was Daisy, who just abjectly refused to be ignored. She was grateful for them both. They kept her from sinking too deep into her restaurant.

"It's also why I'm here, fetching you, instead of stuffing my face with cookies and laughing at Daisy's recount of her ride in a golf cart through the jungle. Go put away whatever it is you're making and get your stuff."

"But I—" She motioned toward the kitchen, glancing back.

"No buts, Sarafina. I haven't had an evening away from Sloan in months. I want cookies, wine, and lots of laughs with my two best friends. Your workaholic tendencies are not going to get in the way of that."

Sara giggled, relenting. She motioned Marci inside. "Fine. But when I act like a zombie early next week because I had to get up super early to make pie crust because I didn't get it made tonight, remember it's your fault." She cast a smile over her shoulder as they walked deeper into the kitchen.

Marci snickered. "Duly noted." Her smile fell away as she took in the mess. "Oh, boy." She heaved a sigh and shrugged out of her coat, hanging it over a wire shelf. "You finish portioning that out. I'll start cleaning up."

"You don't have to help me." Sara moved to the bowl of meatloaf mixture and thrust her hands back in.

Marci snorted. "Yes, I do. Or we'll be here all night. Cookies, wine and BFFs, remember?"

Sara laughed. "Yeah. Okay, thanks."

She quickly added the rest of the ingredients to the bowl and kneaded everything together. Before she started, she'd greased several roasting pans, so she portioned the meatloaf into them, then covered them with plastic wrap. As she carried the last one into the cooler, Marci put the final load of dishes through the dishwasher. Sara grabbed her disinfectant and wiped down the table.

"Is that it?" Marci glanced around.

"Yep."

"Awesome, let's go. Do you want to ride with me or follow?"

"I'll follow you. I have to be back here in the morning, so even if I sleep there, I need to have a way back at an ungodly hour."

Marci chuckled. "Okay."

Sara grabbed her coat and purse from the office, and they left. In her car, Sara cranked the heat and turned on her butt warmer, having forgot—again—to use the remote start and warm up her car. She'd blame it on the rush job, but she forgot when she wasn't rushed.

Pulling out of the parking lot, she followed Marci out of town and up the winding mountain road to the Stone Creek. Half an hour later, they drove through the gates and up to the house, parking in the long driveway.

Lights blazed in the lower level of the house. As she and Marci neared the front door, Sara could hear music and laughter coming from inside. Marci opened the door, and the music swelled. Sharing an amused look, they followed the sound into the living room. Asa belted out the melody to the song playing through the speakers while he waltzed around the room. Daisy stood on his feet, laughing hysterically as he held her close and whirled.

He spotted them on a turn through the room, and paused, grinning widely. "Hey."

Daisy stepped off his feet, stumbling slightly, her balance still off from the injuries she sustained in her car accident. Asa steadied her, then picked up her cane from where it rested on the couch and handed it to her.

"It's about time you got here." Daisy walked over to the stereo and turned the volume down.

"Yeah, well, *someone* was elbow deep in ground beef when I found her." Marci hooked a thumb at Sara.

"I forgot. I'm sorry." Sara held her hands up near her shoulders. "But I'm ready to hear about this golf cart adventure."

Asa laughed. "And on that note, I'll see you later, sweetness." He gave Daisy a quick kiss, waved to them, then left the room.

"Is he going to hang out with your husband?" Sara looked at Marci.

She nodded. "Sloan should be asleep, so I think they're going to watch a basketball game on TV or something." Her husband, Chet, was home with their nine-month-old son.

"Where's your mom and Silas?" Sara asked.

"Billings. They wanted to give us some space so we could adjust to being in the house as a married couple." Daisy grinned. "I'm glad, because it means we get to practice being quiet."

Sara laughed. "How's that going?"

"The practice part is great. The being quiet part, not so much. We might have to add some soundproofing." Her mouth pulled, and she shrugged. "Anyway," she tamped her cane on the hard floor. "Who's ready for some cookies?"

"Me." Sara raised a hand and spun on her heel, heading for the kitchen. Just because she forgot about their plans didn't mean she wasn't ready now for chocolate. Especially since no one made chocolate chip cookies like Daisy.

They all dove into the plate on the counter. Marci grabbed a bottle of wine from the rack on the wall and poured them each a glass.

"So, tell us about this golf cart." Marci wiped a chocolate smear from the corner of her lip. "Chet wouldn't tell me anything. Just that I should ask you."

Daisy rolled her eyes. "No matter what anyone says, it was not my fault."

Sara paused, lips around her cookie. She bit off the chunk and stuffed it into her cheek so she could talk. "Oh, this should be epic."

"Agreed. Spill." Marci picked up her wineglass and took a sip.

Daisy giggled. "Okay. So, we decided to take a tour through the area the resort had that was kind of like an animal preserve. It has this nice concrete road going through it, which was perfect because walking long distances still sucks. Anyway, we took one of the golf carts—Asa was driving—and we stopped because there was a troop of monkeys making a ruckus in the trees, and we wanted to get a better look. We got out and I left my cane on the seat—I had Asa there, we weren't walking more than a few feet, I was fine."

"What happened?" Sara leaned forward and picked up a second cookie.

"We were staring up at the trees, watching them leap from limb to limb, when we heard a clatter behind us. We turned around, and one of them had jumped into the golf cart and had my cane."

"Oh, geez." Marci sipped her wine. "What did you do?"

"I elbowed Asa and told him to do something, so he crept forward, talking to this monkey all soft-like. It cocked its head and did that monkey chatter thing Macaques do. Then it banged the damn thing on the frame, which startled it, but only for a moment. The next thing I knew, it smacked everything it could, using it like a bloody drumstick."

"Oh, no," Marci said.

"Yeah. Because that drew the attention of all his buddies. They swarmed us, all of them wanting to know what he had. One of the bigger ones ran up and just took it from him and hopped into the road. That set them all off and it was a free-for-all. They took off back into the trees." She held up her cane and looked at it. "Asa had to buy me a new cane."

Sara arched an eyebrow and grinned. "Is that why it's glittery pink now? I thought you just painted your old one."

Daisy grinned. "I did paint it, but it's not the old one. We found a man on the street who was making figurines out of wood. Asa asked him to make me a cane. He whittled this out in a few hours, but he didn't have any varnish, so we found a place to buy paint, and they had pink glitter spray paint."

Sara and Marci laughed.

"I told Asa I'm going to put this thing in our closet once I can get around without it, then bring it out once I'm old and gray and need to use it again. I'll be the coolest grandma on the block." She laughed, joining in with her friends.

Taking a drink of her wine, Sara felt herself finally start to relax. Marci was right. She worked too damn much. She shouldn't forget her friends, and it shouldn't take her almost an hour to just start to unwind.

But she didn't know any other way to live. She didn't have a family to speak of around here anymore. Her parents were states away, and she was an only child. Until recently, Marci was her only real friend—all the others moving away for better jobs, or just falling out of touch as Sara threw herself into her business.

And men were few and far between. It wasn't like there were many prospects in Pine Ridge. She knew all the ones her age and had for years. Which meant she knew all their secrets and bad habits.

She could do better, though. Be a better friend. She might not get what Marci and Daisy had with Chet and Asa, but she could still live a full life. She did live a full life. And she was content with what she had.

Really?

She lifted her wineglass again to disguise the frown that formed as her conscience had its say. She smacked it in the face and shoved it back in its box. It could stay there. She *was* happy. She didn't need a man or a family. They were just icing on her already delicious cake.

But you like frosting...

She rolled her eyes at her thoughts and picked up a third cookie.

Two

Car horns and shouts assaulted James O'Malley's ears as he stepped out the front door of his apartment building. He tugged his coat tighter around himself to ward off the brisk Chicago wind and hurried to the curb to hail a cab. A taxi pulled over, and he climbed in, giving the cabbie an address downtown. He stared out the window, preoccupied with thoughts of the coming meeting with his agent. He was two months behind on his next book, and Charlie was calling him on the carpet about it.

It wasn't like he planned to be so far behind on his writing. His sister, Daisy, had been in a car accident, then she got married. He'd been busy. And distracted. Charlie knew all that, but this meeting was to remind James he had obligations to meet. Publishers to satisfy. It was only his past success that granted him the leeway he'd already received. But their patience was running thin.

The steely gray sky passed in a blur as the cab drove deeper into Chicago. The forecast called for snow. Again. It was only mid-November, but they'd already had several snowfalls. The curse of living next to Lake Michigan. James was ready for spring. Or to move to a warmer climate.

At least he didn't have to shovel. That was one perk of apartment living. Two of his brothers had houses in the suburbs. Sometimes—especially when his upstairs neighbor had a party—he wished he lived in a house, but then he remembered he'd have to mow and shovel snow and decided he was happy where he was.

A horn blared as the cab made an abrupt lane change and pulled up to the curb. James paid the driver and got out, jogging into the building. He took the elevator to the tenth floor.

"Hello, Mr. O'Malley."

One side of James's mouth tipped up as the receptionist greeted him. He sauntered forward to lean against her desk. "Hi, Jane."

The young woman blushed and giggled before schooling her features into a more professional mask. "I'll let Charlie know you're here."

He let his smile bloom and nodded. "Thank you."

Her smile peeked out again as she picked up the phone.

James wandered over to the waiting area and sat, resting an ankle atop his knee. He stared down the hall to his right, willing Charlie to appear. He just wanted to get this over with.

"So, how have you been?" Jane asked.

He glanced over to see her peering above her tall desk.

"Can't complain. Busy." As much as he flirted with her, he had no interest in getting involved with his agent's receptionist. She was pretty, but much too young for him. There was a time it wouldn't have mattered, but at thirty-six, he wasn't interested in fleeting trysts anymore.

"James."

At the sound of Charlie's voice, he looked to his right. His agent, Charlie Mills, stood in the mouth of the hallway. He stood smiling at her. "Hello. You look lovely as always, Charlie." And she did. His agent was a beautiful woman. The ivory pantsuit and blue peep-toe heels she wore only emphasized that.

She rolled her eyes. "Cut the crap." She gestured with her head down the hallway, her red ponytail bobbing. "Come on."

James blew out a breath and followed her down the hall into her office.

"Have a seat." She pointed to a chair across from her desk.

He sank into it, crossing his ankle over his knee again. She settled behind her desk, folding her hands over the blotter.

"So. You know why you're here." It wasn't a question.

"Yeah. And I don't know why you called me down here. I told you in my last email I was working on the book. You'll have the first five chapters soon."

"Soon was a week ago, James. It was due eight weeks before that."

"I know." He folded his hands in his lap and looked out the window. She didn't have the best view. Just more buildings.

Charlie sighed. "Look, I just need something, okay? How close are you?"

James scratched the back of his head, scrunching his face. Boy, he didn't want to answer that question.

"James."

The warning note in her voice had him blowing out a breath. He wondered if she got that tone from her ex-Marine husband or if it came naturally. "I have a chapter. And a rough outline."

Her eyebrows shot up. "That's it?"

He nodded. "Yeah. I know it's not a lot."

She scoffed. "You got that right. The whole book is due in three months. Can you make up the time?"

"Yes." And he could. If he could concentrate. After all the

crap that happened in the last few months, it had scrambled his ability to focus.

"Then do it. I don't care what you have to do, whether it's lock yourself in your apartment, take a trip somewhere—hell, you could take a trip to the moon for all I care, so long as you finish that book." She sat forward. "You're a moneymaker for your publishing house, so they're giving you some wiggle room. This meeting is just a reminder that if you don't submit a finished manuscript by the deadline in three months, you have to return your advance."

"I'm aware." It was spelled out in his contract.

"It also means you'll have a hard time finding another publishing deal."

His mouth flattened. She was just piling it on today. None of this was anything he didn't already know. It sucked to have it shoved in his face, though. "I know."

"Good. So, we have an understanding, yes? You're going to do whatever's necessary to write that book, right? Because I don't have to tell you, I don't appreciate having my chain jerked around and then not get paid."

He grinned. "So I can jerk your chain as long as you get your money?"

A smile quirked one corner of her mouth. "Shut up, jackass. Go write your book."

James laughed and stood. "Been great talking to you as always, Charlie." He extended a hand over her desk.

She rose and took it, her expression turning serious. "Whatever's going on in that pretty head of yours, fix it. Before it takes you down."

He inhaled, nodding. "I will." Releasing her hand, he turned and walked out of her office, his face morphing into a frown. The question was, how?

James's phone rang as he exited the building. Glancing at the screen, he raised a hand to hail a cab. His brother Ian's name appeared. He answered as a taxi pulled up, and he got in.

"Hey, what's up?"

"Nori called. Seems Lance filed for custody of Olive."

"What?" His cousin Sofie divorced her husband earlier in the year and put the bastard in jail for abuse. He wasn't even supposed to be out yet. "Isn't he still in jail?"

"Nope. Apparently, he was released about a month ago because of overcrowding."

James scoffed.

"Yeah. Anyway, Sofie and Olive left the Stone Creek and went down to Colorado with a friend of Asa's, Knox Duvall. Lance showed up in Pine Ridge, and Sofie was worried he would try to kidnap Olive. Then the custody papers showed up. Nori said Sofie and Knox are getting married to help fight it."

Married? James stared out the window for a moment in stunned silence. "Why would she need to get married to fight it? How does Lance carry more weight as an abusive ex-con than she does as a loving mother?"

"Because he got his job back and found himself a fiancée. Some finance manager for a bank who lives in their old building. He's trying to paint Sofie as unfit."

"No judge will believe that. Sofie's a great mom."

"I know that, but if Lance buys off the judge, it won't matter. Anyway, Silas hired her one of the best family lawyers he and Asa could find. That's not the entire reason I called, though."

"Oh?" James frowned.

"With Sofie gone and Nori and Silas going to Colorado for the wedding, Daisy could use some help. You're the only one of us with a flexible schedule. Do you think you could fly out there and help her out until Nori gets back after Thanksgiving?"

James closed his eyes and leaned his head against the seat for a second. "This is bad timing, Ian. I just got reamed out by my agent because I haven't submitted anything on my next book. The publishing house is threatening to revoke my advance if I don't deliver the manuscript on time."

Ian paused. "How long do you have?"

"Three months."

"Why are you worrying? You've written books in less than a month before."

"Yeah, but this one's different."

"How so?"

"Nothing's coming to me. It's a new series, so that means new characters, and I just can't get a handle on the guy." And it was driving him crazy. Every time he sat down to write, he never got more than a few paragraphs because he couldn't connect with his character.

"Maybe this is perfect timing, then. Could be you just need a change of scenery?"

James snorted. "I've had a change of scenery recently, remember? We were all out west for Daisy's wedding."

"Right, but we were there to party, not for you to work."

His frown returned. He had a point. Maybe staring at something other than his office walls would do him good. "Fine." He blew out a breath. "I'll fly out today."

Three

Gravel crunched under the tires of his rented SUV as James turned into the Stone Creek's driveway. He pulled up to the gate and pressed the call button on the video intercom.

"James? What are you doing here?" Daisy's voice came over the line. He couldn't see her, but he could hear the frown and surprise in her voice.

"Ian called. Said you could use some help." He held up a hand and smiled at the camera. "Here I am."

"You couldn't have called first?"

His smile died. "Daisy, just let me in. It's been a long day."

"Fine," she growled.

The gate rumbled open, and he drove through, heading up the half-mile lane to the house. He pulled in front of the far garage bay, hoping he wasn't blocking anyone in, and got out.

"Oh, God." He stretched, ecstatic to be out of the car. He was tired of sitting. With a sigh, he opened the liftgate and removed his suitcase, then walked across the drive and up the porch steps.

The door swung open before he could knock. Daisy's green-eyed glare met him.

He smiled at her, not letting it get to him. "Hiya, Sis."

She rolled her eyes and stepped back. He walked inside. Asa came out of the kitchen and held out a hand. James shook it.

"This is a surprise," Asa said.

James shrugged. "Daisy needed help."

"I do not need help. It's ten days."

"It's not a bad idea, sweetness. You're still recovering. James can do the stuff that still gives you problems, like carrying laundry baskets."

Daisy turned to glare at her new husband. "That's what I have you for."

He grinned. "Is that all I'm good for?"

James waved a hand as Asa's eyes heated. "Yuck. No. None of that. Daisy, I'm here, so deal with it."

She huffed. "I should send you packing."

He crossed his arms and raised an eyebrow.

"But you're the least annoying of the six of you, and I know Ian will talk one of the others into coming if I send you home, so fine. You can stay." She waved a finger in his face. "But no bossy business. I know my limits. Clear?"

"As crystal. I'm not here to step on your toes. I just want to help. It also has the added benefit of getting me out of my apartment. Writer's block has hit me hard. Maybe the Montana air will clear my head."

She studied him a moment, then nodded. "Okay. There are leftovers in the kitchen if you're hungry."

That eyebrow winged upward again. "What kind of leftovers?"

"Nothing fancy. Spaghetti."

"There are cookies too," Asa added. "Chocolate chip."

James pushed his suitcase against the entryway wall. "You don't have to tell me twice. I've missed your cookies."

Daisy smiled the first genuine smile James had seen from her since he arrived. "I'm sure you do. You eat almost as many as Asa does."

"They're good cookies." James walked ahead of her into the kitchen, then paused when he realized he didn't know where anything was.

Asa went to a cabinet and took out a plate, handing it to him. "Spaghetti's in the fridge. Cookies are in the cookie jar."

James's mouth watered. He really had missed his sister's cooking. He smiled at them both. "Thanks."

Four

The cowbell strapped to the door clanged as it opened. Sara Katsaros peeked out from the kitchen and smiled as she saw her friend, Daisy Mitchell, walking toward the counter. "Hey, girl. Give me a sec."

Daisy waved a hand and perched on a stool. "Take your time."

Sara ducked back into the kitchen to finish the meal she was preparing for another customer. Her morning cook, Melody, called in sick with the flu, so she was pulling double-duty.

Sliding a spatula under the pancake on the griddle, she lifted the edge to check if it was done. The perfect golden-brown tone met her. She scooped it up and set it atop the stack on the plate at her workstation, then added two slices of bacon and the scrambled eggs staying warm at the back of the griddle. Picking up the small pitcher of maple syrup, she pushed through the swinging doors to the diner and went to the end of the counter.

"Here you go, Bob. Can I get you anything else?" She set

the plate down in front of the grizzled old man who came into her diner twice a week for breakfast.

He shook his head. "I'm good, thanks."

"Okay. Let me know if you need something." She smiled at him, then turned away, strolling down the counter to Daisy. "Hey. What brings you in here so early?"

Daisy sighed. "James showed up last night."

Sara's eyes widened, and her heartbeat increased. "Your brother?" She wiped at a non-existent speck of dirt on the counter as she gathered herself. That man was pure sin in a dark Irish package. He had blue eyes the color of the Caribbean Sea and hair so black it shone blue in the light. And that body... He sure didn't look like a writer. The dark gray suit he wore for the wedding emphasized his powerful physique. She hadn't been able to stop imagining what his shoulders would look like naked. As well as other parts.

She felt her cheeks heat and shut down that line of thinking. Fantasizing about one of the asshats who made Daisy's life miserable for so long was not productive. Hot or not, she refused to give him the time of day, let alone allow him to take up space in her brain.

"Yeah. Ian called him and asked him to come out to help while Nori and Silas are in Colorado."

Sara rolled her eyes, making Daisy giggle.

"I already told him he better watch it."

"Like that will happen. Your brothers can't help themselves."

Daisy shrugged. "We'll see. They've been good about leaving me be." Her mouth twisted. "It probably helps that I have Asa. They think I have someone to 'take care of me.'" She air-quoted the words and shook her head.

"James has always hovered the least. We're the closest in age. He'd just turned eighteen when Mom and Dad died; then he went off to college a few months later. He was the only one not living in Chicago for the first few years after their deaths. I remember once he tried to contradict something Ian told me to do. Ian told him he didn't know what he was talking about and to shut up. James never tried to stop him after that. Especially since the others sided with Ian. I'd get some sympathetic looks, though. And he never tried to set me up with anyone."

"It doesn't excuse him for not standing up for you. For not trying to help you be your own person."

"No, but I've made peace with my brothers. They respect my boundaries now. Usually." Her mouth tilted.

Sara cocked an eyebrow. "That's why you're here at the crack of nine? Because your brothers respect your boundaries?"

Daisy giggled again. "I guess I needed to vent a little about them hovering." She held her fingers up millimeters apart. "But I also needed to get some groceries and didn't want to go out later. It's supposed to snow again."

"Don't remind me." Sara wrinkled her nose. "It's not even Thanksgiving and I'm already sick of winter."

"James said it's been snowing in Chicago too. He was kinda pissed he didn't get away from it."

Sara snorted. "He came to Montana. What did he expect?"

"I know." Daisy grinned, shaking her head. "Wishful thinking, I guess. Anyway, can I have a banana walnut muffin to go? I need to get to the grocery and head home before James decides to start tackling my chore list."

"What's wrong with him doing some of your chores? Isn't that why he's here?" Sara picked up a pair of tongs and opened the display case containing muffins and donuts.

"Theoretically, yes. But I think he agreed more because he needed a change of scenery so he could focus. He's got a book due in a few months and hasn't even really started. I don't want him working on my stuff any more than necessary. He needs to focus on his writing. I'm fine."

Sara bagged the muffin and handed it to Daisy, taking the five-dollar-bill she passed her in return. "Well, I'd still make him work for his room and board." She smiled, ringing up the sale.

"Oh, I will. I was thinking of starting him out in the chicken coop. Cookie did it this morning, but tomorrow? All bets are off. He can trudge through the snow to feed the birds and collect the eggs. I'll stay nice and toasty inside."

Sara laughed and passed Daisy her change. She'd pay to be a fly on the wall to watch that man collect eggs and wade through chicken poop. "It might be worth it to put your winter gear on and follow him out there to take pictures. For blackmail purposes later."

"That's a good idea." Daisy laughed and rose from her stool. "Plus, I'm sure our brothers would love to see that he's pulling his weight. Thanks for the muffin." She waved with the bag in her hand. "I'll see you later."

"You bet." Sara waved back. The bell clanged again as Daisy left. Picking up her rag, she walked around the counter to clean off a couple of tables, trying not to think about the Irish devil staying at the Stone Creek. She had a weakness for men like him. Self-assured. Cocky. Gorgeous.

In her experience, those men also turned out to be players and jerks. She didn't need that in her life. Not anymore.

Sara stacked dishes and scrubbed the table, scowling. Why was she giving James O'Malley any brainpower? He didn't deserve it. After Thanksgiving, he wouldn't even be around anymore. Huffing, she picked up the stack of dishes and headed for the kitchen, determined not to think about him.

～

Fat snowflakes fell from the sky to land in James's hair as he climbed out of his car. He glanced at the clouds, realizing he should have listened to Daisy and stayed on the ranch. Or asked her to pick up some groceries for him. She'd asked if he wanted anything before she left, but he'd been barely awake and said he'd go later. She warned him it was supposed to snow, but it hadn't truly registered in his foggy brain.

James shut the car door and hurried into the store, grabbing a cart. He needed to get his groceries and get out. The road to town was a winding one, and he did not want to be on it in the middle of a snowstorm.

Aiming the cart toward the produce section, he steered it through the aisles, finding what he came for as well as a few extras. Getting past writer's block required junk food and copious amounts of caffeine. At the register, he eyed the heavily falling snow through the front windows. His drive home was going to suck.

The clerk handed him his receipt, the young girl eyeing him with a curious frown. He knew she probably didn't see many outsiders, especially this time of year, but he didn't enlighten her about his identity. He wouldn't be in town long enough for it to matter. Muttering a thanks, he looped the grocery bags over his wrist and left.

Outside, he pressed the button on his remote to open the liftgate and set the bags inside. Items stowed, he shut the door, then got in the car, using the wipers to clear the snow from his windshield. There was already nearly an inch on the ground.

He shifted the car into gear and pulled out of the parking lot, praying he didn't slide off a mountain on his way back to the Stone Creek. The roads weren't too bad yet, but he knew that might change once he climbed in elevation.

Fifteen minutes into his return drive, it did just that. Snow coated the roadway, crunching under his tires, and he slowed. "Why didn't I listen to Daisy? Did I really need Chunky Monkey ice cream today?" Growling at his own stupidity, he clenched the wheel, steering the car around a bend.

"Shit!" He hit his brakes at the sight of an elk standing in the middle of the road. His car fishtailed. James steered into the skid, but the road surface was at an angle and he continued to slide. He let off the brake and turned the wheel, sliding into the ditch hood first instead of rolling in sideways. The car rocked to a stop, the seatbelt holding him in place.

"Fucking snow. I hate winter." He put the car in reverse, but the angle was too steep. His tires just spun on the snow-covered ground. Grumbling under his breath, he fished his phone from the cupholder to call his sister. She would love this. He'd probably never hear the end of it.

He found her number and touched the call icon, but it wouldn't connect. "Dammit!" He didn't have a signal; not even to text. Shutting off the engine, he got out and scrambled up the embankment to the road. The elk stood on the opposite side of the road in the trees now. It stared at him. He glared back, then lifted his phone, hoping he could get a bar or two. Even if he only got enough to send a text, it would be better than nothing. At least someone would know he was stuck. Eventually.

But the signal indicator stayed stubbornly empty. His breath puffed out in front of him as he emptied his lungs with a huff. Indecision chewed at his gut. He looked back at his car, debating whether to get back in and hope someone came along, or whether to start walking. He was five miles from town. If he stayed in the grass, he could run. The snow wasn't too deep yet, and he'd been sensible enough to wear some decent shoes. On the other hand, if the snow fell any harder, he could end up in a world of trouble.

He swiped a hand down his face. But what happened if he didn't? He didn't pass a single car on his way to town. What were the chances someone would come along before he froze? Jaw working, he stared down the road into the swirling snow, then looked at his car. His white car. With the snowfall increasing, no one would ever see it. Not with the headlights facing into the ditch.

"Aargh!" He tipped his head back, closing his eyes as he came to a decision. He had a better chance running back to town than sitting in his car. It would be hours before anyone found him, even if Daisy sent out a search party. And there was no guarantee anyone would see him through the snow. Or could even get down the mountain to look for him.

Growling again, he jogged back to his car, only to have his feet slide on the roadway. Arms windmilling, he managed to stay upright and get to the vehicle without any bruises. Wrenching open the door, he shut off the engine and pocketed the keys. He wished he had a blanket. It would help cut the wind around his legs. His coat and gloves were warm, though. He was a Chicagoan, after all.

With one last glance at the car, he flipped his hood up and set off at a quick jog through the frozen grass.

Five

Snow, carried by the icy wind, blasted Sara's face as she stepped outside. Shivering as it hit her neck, exposed by her ponytail, she pulled the door closed and slid the key into the lock, twisting it. She'd closed early today. Once the snow started, business died. There was no sense in keeping herself or her staff at the diner when no one was leaving their homes. The forecast called for six to eight inches over the next several hours.

She glanced at the sky as she used the remote start button on her fob, then opened the rear driver's side door to get her snowbrush. If it kept snowing like this, they would end up with far more than that. Clearing the windshield, she put the brush away and climbed in, turning on the seat warmer after buckling up. The rest of her might be cold on the ride home, but her butt would be toasty.

Thankfully, her house wasn't too far away. Pine Ridge was small, and she lived just outside of town on several acres. One day, she'd find the time to put in the large garden she wanted as well as get a few animals. Right now, she was too busy with her restaurant to take care of even the tiniest farmstead by herself.

Sara pulled out of the lot, snow crunching under her tires as she drove out of town. Even with her four-wheel drive and snow tires, she could still feel the wheels slip when she slowed. As she passed the corporation limit, she didn't speed up. The county roads were usually pretty terrible until a plow went down them, which, from the looks of things, hadn't happened yet. It didn't help that she couldn't see very far ahead, either. The snow came down in thick sheets, and the wind swirled it around, taking visibility down to just yards.

It was the lack of visibility that nearly made her miss the figure jogging along the side of the road. Her brain registered a person waving their arms, but she didn't slow until she was well past the figure in the dark coat.

Heart thudding in her chest, she put the car in reverse and backed up. Who the hell was walking out here in a snowstorm?

The figure came into view, and she could tell it was a man from his size. She came to a stop and rolled down her window. He stumbled forward, his gloved hands landing on the windowsill. She looked over into bright blue eyes.

"James? Jesus, you look like you're freezing! Get in."

He hurried around the hood to climb into the passenger seat. Sara pushed the button to turn on his seat warmer as he tugged off his gloves and pushed his hood back. He glanced at her, and she noted his chapped cheeks and the icicles hanging off the tips of his hair around his face.

"What are you doing out here?" Her eyes widened. "Were you in an accident? Are you hurt? Is anyone else?"

He shook his head. "I'm fine. I slid off the road up the mountain. I couldn't get a signal on my phone, and I was closer to town than the ranch. God, it's cold!" His teeth chattered, and he put his hands in front of the vents. They were white. He glanced at her. "Sara, right?"

She nodded. "We need to get you warm. You might have some frostbite on your hands and face. Buckle up if you can." She put the car in drive and crept forward again.

"I'm glad you came along. How far am I from town?" His hands shook as he fumbled with the belt, finally locking it into place.

"About two miles or so. We should be coming up on the turnoff to my road soon, and it's about three miles out of town. How far did you walk?"

"I jogged, actually. In the grass so I wouldn't fall. I think I went about two-and-a-half miles." He blew on his hands and rubbed them together.

Sara could see the fine tremors running through his body. She gave him a side glance, not wanting to take her eyes off the road. "You're lucky you didn't get lost."

"I followed the road."

"You should have stayed in your car."

"To freeze? No thanks. We both know no one was coming down that road until the plows went through. And they might have just buried me deeper, making me harder to see. My rental's white."

She slowed as she saw the stop sign through the swirling snow and made the turn onto her road.

"Where are we going?"

"My house."

"What? Can you just take me to town? I'm sure I'll be able to get a signal once we're closer to civilization and I'll call my sister."

"No one's coming to get you in this, James. And I'm not turning around. The roads are already terrible." She inhaled a breath and chanced another glance at her passenger. "You can stay with me until the weather clears."

"Sara—"

"No arguing. I'm not going back to town. Unless you want to get out and jog the rest of the way, you're coming home with me."

He looked at her from the corner of his pretty eyes. Sara did her best to ignore him and continued to creep down her road.

"So," James sighed, "how far away is your place?"

"We're almost there." She adjusted her grip on the wheel, slowing as her neighbor's mailbox appeared. She didn't want to miss her driveway. The Coulson's mailbox didn't come into view until she was practically on top of it.

They crawled the last half mile until her mailbox emerged from the heavy snow, and she made the turn into her driveway. She pushed the button on her garage door opener and pulled into the garage, then cut the engine. A glance at James revealed he was still mostly frozen. The ice had started to thaw off his hair, but his skin was still pale except for his cheeks, and he still shivered.

"Come on. Let's get you warmed up." She opened her door and climbed out.

He nodded, following her from the car. She let them into the house, shedding her coat and dumping her purse on the bar as they passed through the kitchen. Sara didn't bother with her shoes. Her priority was getting James warm. The best way she knew to do that was to put him in the shower.

She led him down a short hallway to the guest bath, flipping on the light as they entered. "If you give me your clothes, I'll put them in the dryer for you. I'd offer you something different, but I don't have anything that will fit you. Not even my bathrobe." She ran her eyes over his tall, muscular form, then spun away to turn on the shower, setting it to barely lukewarm. As cold as he was, hot water would hurt too much.

"That should be good." She glanced back to see him

fumbling with the zipper on his coat. "Do you need some help?"

"No," he growled. When his fingers failed to grasp the tiny fob again, he sighed and looked at her. "Yes."

Without a word, Sara stepped forward and pulled down the zipper on his coat, helping him shrug out of it. "Can you get your shirt off on your own?"

He nodded and grasped the hem, pulling it up over his head. Sara's mouth went dry as he revealed the hard body beneath. She did her best to keep her eyes on his face and not the happy trail splitting his abdomen to disappear beneath the waistband of his jeans. The man was in the early stages of hypothermia and didn't need her ogling him.

It was damn hard, though. Especially when his hands dropped to his waist to unbutton his pants. She swallowed around the lump in her throat and bent to pick up his coat and shirt.

"Dammit!"

She straightened, holding his things. "What's wrong?"

"I can't unfasten my jeans. My hands won't work right."

Oh, frick. Sara took a steadying breath and set his things on the counter, then stepped in front of him. She slid her fingers into his waistband. His chilly skin helped her to push away some of her attraction. Stripping him of his clothes wasn't about pleasure; it was about survival.

She twisted her hands, unfastening the button, then drew down the zipper and stepped back. "Can you get your shoes off?"

He shook his head, his jaw working as he tried to keep his teeth from chattering. Goosebumps stood out in harsh relief all over his exposed skin.

"Sit." She pointed to the closed toilet. He lowered himself down, and she crouched in front of him, untying his boots and tugging them off his feet. She took his socks off, then stood. "I'm going to step out into the hallway. Take off the rest of your clothes and pass them out to me." She whirled, taking a towel from the linen cabinet. Setting it on the counter, she reached for the doorknob.

"Wait. My sister. I need to call her, so she doesn't worry."

"I have a landline. I'll call her for you. Get warm." She turned the knob and left the room. Once in the hall, she closed her eyes and blew out a breath. Damn. Sara clenched her jaw, stuffing the memory of his naked chest and abs into an airtight box. She didn't need that image eroding her defenses to him. He'd be on his way back to Chicago soon enough, where she'd never have to worry about how he made her feel again.

∼

James shoved his pants and boxer-briefs down his frozen thighs and stepped out of them. He did not want to get in that shower, but knew he had to. He could tell from the lack of steam building in the room, the water was barely warm. But it was still going to hurt like the dickens.

Opening the door a crack, he passed his pants to Sara, then closed it and pulled back the shower curtain. With a deep breath, steeling himself, he stepped into the tub. Pain shot through his toes as water sluiced over them. The muscles in his arms and back clenched and his hands throbbed. He groaned and rested his head against the tile wall, waiting for the pain to subside.

Gradually, some of the feeling came back to his limbs, so he increased the temperature, wading through a fresh wave of pain each time he raised the heat. When he could stand beneath the hot spray without clenching his teeth, he shut off the water and dried himself with the towel Sara left out for him. He felt human again.

A glance in the mirror revealed he didn't look that way,

though. Dark circles colored the area beneath his eyes, and his mouth drooped with fatigue. He might be warm now, but his jog through the cold left him exhausted. His body felt like he carried an extra hundred pounds on his shoulders. He hoped Sara had a place he could crash. Sleep sounded heavenly.

Wrapping the towel around his waist, he exited the bathroom in search of his hostess. "Sara?"

"In here."

He turned toward the kitchen. She glanced up as he entered, her eyes going wide before she schooled her face.

"Um," she cleared her throat. "Your clothes are on the table over there." She nodded toward the dining table to his left. "I made you some soup too. And there's coffee." She pointed at the coffeepot beside her.

"Thanks." He walked over and picked up his clothes. They were still warm from the dryer. "I'll go get dressed and be back."

She nodded, and he left, returning to the bathroom to dress. Once he was presentable, he wandered back to the kitchen.

"Feel better?" she asked, pouring two cups of coffee.

"Much. Thank you."

"You're welcome. Have a seat, and I'll bring your food over."

"I can carry it."

She glared at him. "Just sit, would you?" She picked up a blue ceramic bowl and a coffee mug. "You're as bad as your sister."

He couldn't help but grin at that. The O'Malley stubbornness was the reason Daisy ended up out here to begin with. But he wouldn't fight her about this. He was too tired. Pulling out a chair at the table, he sank into it. She set the bowl and mug down in front of him.

"Thanks."

She nodded, then retrieved the other mug and sat down across from him.

"Did you call Daisy?"

"Yes. She said she's glad you're safe and that next time, you should listen to her."

He barked out a laugh. "Yeah. She warned me it was going to snow. I thought I could make it back before it got too bad. I probably would have, too, if it weren't for the damn elk in the road."

"That's how you ended up in the ditch?"

He nodded. "I came around the bend, and it was just standing in the middle of the road. With the slant of the roadway, I didn't stand a chance." He dipped his spoon into the soup and took a bite, loving the warmth that spread through his chest. He was still chilly.

"You're lucky that's the section you went off. It's a lot steeper a couple miles down the road. And that you weren't out there longer. How are your hands?"

He turned his hands over, looking at both sides. There were some small areas of discoloration, but nothing terrible. "They're not bad. Having gloves definitely helped." He flexed his fingers. They felt fine.

"Good. You have a couple of spots on your face."

James touched his cheeks. "Yeah. It's still numb in places. I tried to keep my head down and out of the wind."

"You should probably see a doctor just to be safe, but it doesn't look that bad to me."

"Have you seen much frostbite?" He took another bite of his soup.

"It's inevitable living up here. A lot of my older regulars have frostbite scars."

"Yeah. Silas has some weathering on his face and hands too." He frowned as a thought occurred to him. He needed to make sure Daisy had the proper winter gear, so that didn't happen to her.

"Stop it."

James looked at her. "Stop what?"

"Worrying about your sister. She'll be fine. I'm sure Asa's already bought her everything she needs to protect her skin."

He frowned again, putting his spoon back in his soup. "Well, it won't hurt to check."

She rolled her eyes. "Do you even know what the proper gear is?"

"I'm from Chicago. We have winter there, too, you know."

"Mmm-hmm. Where there's a building everywhere you look. Up here, you're on your own."

"I'm aware."

"Now, yes. But if you truly had been before, you would have worn mittens instead of gloves, had a scarf wrapped around your neck, and a balaclava over your face. Plus, a stocking cap for under your hood. And wool socks on your feet instead of cotton."

"Thank you, teacher." A scowl covered his face, and he took another bite.

"Don't be an ass. Just be better prepared." She stood. "I'm going to make up the spare bedroom for you."

Regret and a touch of shame filled James's chest. He shot a hand out to grab her arm as she walked past. "I'm sorry. I appreciate what you've done for me. I'm not trying to be a jerk. I just—" He blew out a breath. "I just don't like feeling impotent."

A soft smile spread over her pretty face. "No one does. And thank you for apologizing." She nodded her head toward the table. "Finish your soup."

With a nod, he let her go. Feelings he couldn't name swirled in his head as he watched her leave. She did weird things to his insides, but he was too tired to sort out what exactly. He found her pretty, that much he knew, but he didn't think she liked him much. Why, though, he didn't know. They barely spoke in the time he was here for Daisy's wedding or for the few days he was here when she had her accident.

James lifted another spoonful of the vegetable soup to his mouth and did his best to shove thoughts of her from his mind. Whether she liked him or not, it didn't matter. He wouldn't be around long enough for it to make a difference.

Six

The sheet billowed over the mattress as Sara fanned it out to make James's bed. The lights blinked, and she paused. "No, please." She stared at the light fixture, praying it stayed on. It flickered again, then went out and stayed out.

She groaned and put down the sheet. "Dammit!" Gathering the comforter into her arms, she walked back to the living room. James came in from the kitchen.

"Can you start laying wood in the fireplace?" She put the blanket down on the couch. "We're bunking out here tonight unless the power comes back on." Which she highly doubted would happen. Line crews wouldn't be out this way until morning, at least. "I have a generator, but it's only big enough to power my refrigerator and the water pump."

"Sure." He walked over and lifted the screen off the hearth, setting it aside.

Sara used the flashlight on her phone to navigate into the dark kitchen, locating her boots near the garage door.

"Do you need some help?" James's voice carried from the living room.

"No. I'll be right back." She shrugged into her coat, then

went into the garage to get the generator. Thankfully, she kept it fueled and ready to go, so all she had to do was plug it into her electric panel and put it out on the back porch.

Sara slung the rolled cord over her shoulder and picked up the small generator, walking out the back door of the garage to the covered patio that ran the length of her house. She set it a good distance from the exterior wall, then plugged the cord into it and went back inside. Locating the main on the breaker box, she flipped it off and set all the breakers to off, then plugged the generator in and turned on the main and the breaker connected to the generator outlet. She found the breakers for the kitchen and the water pump and turned them on. Closing the panel door, she went back into the house.

It was still considerably warmer inside than outside. The fire should keep it that way, though the temperature would still dip. They were in for a chilly night.

After taking off her coat and boots, she crossed to the pantry to retrieve her emergency supplies. She kept a lantern, a couple of flashlights, and some batteries in a tote for occasions like this. It happened far too often for her liking, but she dealt with it because she enjoyed the solitude of living out here.

"Do you have some matches?" James asked as she walked back into the living room.

"On the wall there, above the wood."

He lifted his phone to shine the flashlight on the wall.

"Did you find the kindling and newspaper?"

"Yep. It's ready. I just need to light it." He took the matches from the decorative box hanging on the wall, then crouched in front of the fire grate and struck one. Touching it to the newspaper, he lit the kindling.

Sara left him to it and went to gather more bedding. She also dug out a selection of board games. It was only six o'clock, so they needed something to pass the time.

"Do you want help?"

"No." She set the stack of games on one end of the couch. "I think I have everything. Unless you want to play cards. Those are in a drawer in the kitchen."

One corner of his mouth lifted. "You don't want to play cards with me, honey. You'll lose."

She lifted a brow. "Cocky much?"

His smile bloomed. "No. Just stating a fact."

"Hmm. What if it's Uno? Still sure of yourself?"

"Bring it, sweet cheeks."

Amusement made her grin. She rolled her eyes and walked toward the kitchen. "Oh, I will." She retrieved the Uno deck and sat down on the floor by the coffee table.

He snatched the cards from her hands. "I don't trust you. I'll shuffle."

"Like I should trust you? You're the one declaring yourself a card shark."

He grinned and kept shuffling. "So, does this happen often?" He gestured around them at their lack of lights, then dealt the cards.

Sara shrugged and picked hers up. "Often enough, I suppose. Especially in weather like this. I'm surprised it stayed on this long with the wind being what it is."

"I'm glad it did. It meant I got a hot shower and warm clothes and didn't die of hypothermia."

"I'd have rolled you up in a bunch of blankets and put you near the fire."

He waggled his eyebrows. "Would you have stripped me naked first?"

Sara's cheeks warmed, and she was thankful for the dim light. "You did fine by yourself once I unfastened all your buttons and zippers."

"It wasn't nearly as fun as if you'd stripped me down too."

She snorted. "Like you'd have cared? You were practically a

popsicle." She rearranged her cards and glanced at the one he turned over.

"Maybe." He shrugged. "Would have been fun to see."

"Does that slick cockiness you project really work on women?" She laid down a blue three.

"Baby, I don't usually even need to talk." He covered her three with a blue seven.

Sara changed the color to red with a red seven. "Of course you don't. Those abs probably make all the easy women just drop their drawers for you."

"So, you noticed." He grinned at her and put a red draw two over her seven.

She tried to ignore the wicked twinkle in his eyes. Her lips twitched, but she pressed them together and drew two cards. "Of course I noticed. You might annoy me, but I'm not dead."

His brow dipped as he laid down a red one. "How do I annoy you?"

Silently, she cursed her big mouth. Why had she said that? She huffed and used her wild card to change the color to yellow. "You just do."

"That's not an answer. I just want to understand. We barely know each other, yet you seem to dislike me." He laid down a yellow eight.

Sara made him draw two. "Can you blame me? You treated your sister like crap for years and you think you're God's gift to women. You're a shallow jerk." She reversed play, skipped him, then laid a yellow five.

He frowned, pausing as he picked up his two cards. "I'm neither, Sara."

She glanced at him, ready to refute his words, but the look in his eyes stopped her. He was sincere. She tilted her head to study him. Had she judged him too quickly?

But what did it matter, really? He'd be gone soon. She blinked and shrugged. "Whatever you say."

He stuffed the cards into his hand, then put down a green five. "How about we talk about something else?"

"Such as?" She laid a green six.

"You." He covered her six with a nine.

"Me? What about me?" All she had left was blue, so she drew a card. She put the green two on the pile.

"Tell me about yourself. You know all about me, but I don't know anything about you." He grinned. "Except you're going to lose." He put down a draw four. "Red."

She resisted the urge to growl and picked up her cards. Most of them were blue.

He put down a red four. "Uno."

"Not so fast." She slapped a blue four over it.

James frowned. "That's not fair."

Sara giggled. "Draw, boy."

"You still didn't tell me about yourself." He picked up a card, wrinkling his nose as it didn't match what he needed.

"What do you want to know?"

"Well, for starters, how about your last name?" He drew a card and laid it down.

"Katsaros. Sarafina Katsaros." She frowned as she studied her hand, then selected a blue six.

"Greek?"

She nodded.

"Okay." He drew another card and added it to his hand. "Tell me something else about you."

"Like?"

He shrugged. "Whatever you want to tell me."

She hummed and put down another card. "Not much to tell, really. I'm an only child. I've lived here since I was fourteen. My parents moved to New Mexico while I was in college, but I didn't want to join them. This is my home. I opened my restaurant with some seed money from my dad and never looked back."

"Where are you from originally?"

"New Mexico. I was born in Santa Fe."

He drew another card, huffing as it didn't match. "What made your family move up here?"

"There's a resort further up the mountain past the Stone Creek. My dad worked for the corporation that owns it and became the manager for a while. About ten years ago, the same position opened at a resort in Taos. Mom works as an accountant from home, so she eagerly packed up her business and followed." She laid another card. "Neither of them liked the winters up here."

"Can't say as I blame them after experiencing it today. But why didn't you want to go?"

Her face pulled as he drew another card and laid it, changing the color to red again. "I made some great friends in high school here, and this place felt like home. It wasn't a difficult decision to come back here and open my diner after college, especially since the only other diner Pine Ridge had closed a few months before I graduated. Though most of those friends have since moved on." She drew another card and grinned. It was a draw four.

"Blue."

He groaned. "I hate you."

Sara giggled with glee as he drew his cards. She waited until he was done, then slapped a draw two down.

"Oh, come on!"

She laid a reverse over it, then another blue card.

Grumbling, he laid a blue card over hers. They battled back and forth until Sara only had one card left. He eyed her, then drew a card, changing the color once more.

"Oh, that's perfect." She laid down her last card and tossed her head back, laughing.

James's mouth flattened, and he threw his cards down.

"Talk about a card shark. That's what I'm going to start calling you: Shark. That was brutal. I swear you cheated."

She laughed again. "I did not."

A corner of his mouth quirked. "Best two out of three?"

Seven

The fire fluttered as wind howled down the chimney. It threw a chill over James's body, and he huddled deeper into his comforter, wishing for an electric blanket. Or electricity in general. Then they'd have real heat and he could sleep in a real bed instead of on a stack of blankets on the floor. His back hurt and his nose was numb again.

He heard Sara sigh, then the rustle of fabric as she sat up on the couch. "Are you okay?"

James blew out a breath and turned over. "I'm fine. Just cold. I never completely thawed out earlier."

There was a brief silence. "I have a teakettle and instant coffee. I can make you some if you want."

A hot drink sounded good, but coffee would just keep him awake. "What about hot chocolate?"

Her low chuckle broke the quiet. "I have that too." She pushed out of her blankets and stood. Her flashlight clicked on, then she left the room.

James stayed where he was. Chills ran through him. If he emerged from his cocoon, he'd just start shivering. He'd wait until the hot cocoa was ready.

Sara came back with two mugs, spoons, a jar with what he assumed was hot chocolate, a teakettle, and an oven mitt. She kneeled in front of the fire and set the kettle on the camping grate she put over the fire earlier.

"Thank you," he mumbled, staring at her back.

She glanced back, her curtain of dark hair falling over one shoulder. "You're welcome. To be honest, I couldn't sleep either. You're right, it's chilly in here and I'm too far from the fire on the couch."

He frowned. "Do you want to trade spots?" He didn't like that she was cold because he took up the space near the fire.

She waved a hand at him. "No. You need the heat more than me. I'll be fine."

James sat up and swung his legs around. "Bullshit. I'll just scoot over. Get your blankets."

"Really, I'm fine."

"Uh-huh. Sure." He rolled his eyes. "Get your blankets. Maybe our combined body heat will keep us warmer."

"That only works if we're sharing the same blankets."

"Well, then maybe we should." His body tightened as he thought about her slender form pressed against his. Her eyes widened as she stared at him. He held her gaze as heat built between them.

The kettle whistled, jolting them apart. He reached for the jar of hot cocoa mix as she put on the oven mitt and took the kettle off the fire.

"How much of this stuff should I use?" James unscrewed the jar lid.

"I usually use three spoonfuls."

He put three heaping spoonfuls of the mix in a mug, then handed it to her. She poured water over it, while he added mix to the second mug, then they traded. She set the kettle on the hearth, then stirred her drink.

James took a sip of his and moaned. "Damn, woman. This

stuff is good." He took another sip. "I take it it's not the Swiss Miss kind?"

She smiled. "No. I make it myself. It's just cocoa powder, dried milk, and some sugar."

"Well, it's delicious."

"Thank you." She took a sip from her mug.

James eyed her over the top of his, noting the shiver that ran through her as she sat there. He set his cup on the hearth and got up.

"Where are you going?"

"You're freezing." He walked over to the couch and pulled her blankets off. Dumping them next to her, he crouched and wrapped the heavy quilt around her shoulders.

She clutched the sides together. "Oh, thank you."

James started to smile, then his gaze met hers. That heat from a few minutes ago surged again. He cleared his throat and looked away, rising to move back to his pile of blankets.

"Tell me something."

He glanced at her. "What?"

"How does a thriller writer from Chicago know how to build a fire?"

"Just because I'm a city slicker doesn't mean I don't know things."

She lifted an eyebrow. "Book research?"

He laughed. "No. I was in Boy Scouts growing up."

"Seriously?"

James nodded and picked up his drink, having settled into his blankets again. "I made Eagle Scout."

Both her brows rose. "For real? I would not have pegged you for that. How did you end up as a writer, then?"

"I got tired of law."

"Wait, you're an attorney?"

"Yes. I haven't practiced in years, though. Once I wrote my first best-seller, I left my job to write full time."

"What kind of law did you practice?"

"Criminal. I worked for the city prosecutor's office."

"Daisy never mentioned any of this."

He shrugged and drank more hot chocolate. "I can't say I'm surprised. I'm betting she didn't do much talking about any of us, other than to say she was pissed at us."

Sara's mouth pulled. "Yeah. She never mentioned Ian was a doctor until she and Asa went to Chicago for that Make-A-Wish thing. I only know you're a writer because I recognized your name."

A smile tilted his mouth. "You read my books?"

She raised her mug and took a drink, looking over it at him with round eyes. "I plead the fifth."

He laughed. "That's a yes. Which one is your favorite?"

Glancing up as she thought, she took another sip of her drink. "Probably the last one. I like how you ended the series. I'm going to miss those characters, though. Daisy said you're working on a new series. That part of the reason you're here is to write. What's it about?"

James groaned and closed his eyes for a moment. "That's the million-dollar question. Literally. I thought I knew, but every time I sit down and try to write, I come up empty."

"Hmm. Maybe it's the character. Have you tried changing your lead? Change up his backstory or something."

"I've thought about that, but the backstory is fine. I just can't get into the plot."

"What is the plot?"

"It's an espionage series."

Sara arched a brow. "Spies? Your last novels were about an Interpol agent chasing international smugglers. Do you know anything about spies?"

"Enough. I've done some research, so I'm not completely winging it."

"But your heart's not in it, is it?"

He sighed. "No. My agent suggested the topic."

"What do *you* want to write?" She reached out and poked his bicep.

"Honestly? A serial killer series. I majored in psychology. For a while, it was a toss-up whether I was going to go to law school or get my Ph.D. The criminal mind is fascinating."

Sara scrunched her nose. "If you say so. Why don't you write that, though?"

"Because it's not what my publisher contracted me for."

"So, go to them and say, this is what I want to write. It's more in your lane, anyway, right?"

He nodded, thinking about what she said. Charlie would be pissed if he changed things on her. Hell, he'd have to go over her head to change his contract. She'd been adamant he write the spy novels. Said they were what was hot.

Sara snapped her fingers. "What about a serial killer spy?"

James frowned. "What do you mean?"

"Most spies are only a few bricks short of being full-blown sociopaths. What if your main character was a true sociopath, and he was a spy?"

"Like Dexter?" he said, mentioning the television character.

"Sort of. But he's not an investigator. Maybe he's a fixer or something. Give him a crisis of morality with a love interest or a friend."

"If he's a true sociopath, he won't put someone else above himself. He won't ever fall in love. Not in the sense a normal person does."

Her mouth twisted. "So maybe he's not a sociopath. He's been brainwashed into thinking what he's doing is right. And what if he's not the spy, but the person the spies are chasing?"

James sat straighter. That had possibilities.

"Everyone loves a reformed villain. And who's writing that kind of book from the villain's perspective?"

Ideas formed in James's head. He wished he had his laptop. Busy building plotlines in his head, he didn't notice Sara get up and return until she put a notebook and a pen in his face. He glanced up, startled.

"I could see the wheels turning." She waved the notebook.

He took it and the pen. "Thanks."

"You're welcome." She settled back into her blankets. "I want an acknowledgement in the book on how I inspired this best-selling series."

James made a humming sound, only listening with half an ear as he scrawled notes and scenes over the paper. He heard her sigh, then giggle softly before she settled into her blanket nest.

As he wrote, his hot chocolate grew cold, but he didn't care. This was the most excited he'd been about a story in months. He didn't care if he didn't sleep tonight. His brain needed to purge all these ideas before he could even try.

Eight

Mug of hot coffee in hand, Sara stood over James, where he slept on the floor by the fireplace. She couldn't believe he wasn't awake with all the noise she'd made getting ready. Not to mention the smell of coffee as she brewed it just feet from his head.

But he needed to get up. The plow had been by to dig her out so she could get to town and open the restaurant. She nudged his hip with her foot. "James. Wake up."

He grumbled and rolled over.

Sara rolled her eyes. He was one of *those* people. She bent down and yanked all the blankets off of him.

"What the hell?" He sat up, blinking against the light coming in from the windows. "Sara? Why did you take my blankets?"

"Because you need to get up. I need to get to town to open the restaurant. You're coming with me."

"Why?"

"Why are you coming with me?"

He yawned and nodded.

"Because I'm going to need help. I'm already short-staffed,

and the waitress who works today lives further from town than I do. She's still snowed-in."

"You want me to wait tables?"

"Or cook. I don't care which." She thrust the coffee mug at him. "Here. Drink this and do whatever you need to do to make yourself presentable. There's an extra toothbrush in the bathroom cabinet."

"How are we supposed to get out? Aren't we snowed-in too?"

"No. The plow drivers know where I live. I have the only restaurant in town, so they make it a priority to dig me out so I can get to work."

"Oh." He yawned again and stood. His dark hair was mussed.

Sara turned away before she thrust her hands in it like she wanted to and mussed it further. "I'm going to go start the snowblower and clear the driveway. Drink your coffee and brush your teeth."

He saluted her. "Yes, ma'am."

She tossed him a grin and walked out of the room. In the kitchen, she put on her coat, hat, and mittens, then clomped out into the garage in the snow boots she put on before she woke up James. Using the chain that bypassed the electric door opener, she raised the garage door. A sea of white met her gaze, but she could see the road cut at the end of her drive. Heaving a sigh, she tucked her scarf around her face, then maneuvered the snowblower to the doorway. She gave the cord a yank to start it, and it roared to life.

At a steady clip, she cleared the top of the drive so she could back her car out and start it. Once she had it running, she walked the rest of her drive, blowing the snow into the yard. She was glad the driveway wasn't terribly long, and that she had it paved several years ago. It still took her fifteen minutes, but at least she didn't need a plow to get down the drive.

Driveway clear, she stowed the snowblower and went back inside. James sat at the dining table, tying his boots.

"I put the fire out, so I'm ready when you are."

Sara swapped out her mittens for gloves, stuffing the other set in her roomy purse. "Let's go, then." She picked up her bag and turned back to the garage. He followed her, shrugging into his coat as they exited the house. "Go ahead and get in the car. I have to shut the door from inside since the power's out."

"I can do that." He paused in the open doorway.

"It'll only take a minute."

"Exactly. Go get in the car."

She huffed, as he didn't give her a chance to protest further. He ducked back inside. Sara went to the car and got in. She saw the door close in the mirror, then James exited the garage.

"It's definitely not any warmer than yesterday," he remarked as he climbed inside. A quick shiver went through him.

Sara put the car in reverse and backed out of the driveway onto the road. "Nope. And it's just as windy. I hope we'll be able to get back in later without having to blow it out again." She shifted into drive and headed for town.

"How long do you think it will be before I can get back to the Stone Creek?"

"Another day or two. The wind is supposed to die tonight and there isn't anymore snow in the forecast."

"Good, because I'm failing in my mission to help Daisy while Nori and Silas are gone."

"At least you conquered your writer's block."

"Thanks for helping, by the way. I don't know why I never thought of flipping the script. I just hope it goes over well."

"I think it will. I'd read it, and I'm sure your fans will too."

"Yes, but will they like it is the better question."

"Well, don't screw it up and they'll like it just fine."

He barked out a laugh. "Got it."

She giggled, slowing to make the turn onto the road into town. The county road was even better than her little side street, and she sped up. It didn't take them long to reach the diner. She parked out back, then let them in through the rear door.

"Do you know how to work a commercial coffeepot?" She flipped on the lights as they entered, glancing back at him.

"I'm sure I can figure it out. They just have a couple of switches, right?"

Sara nodded. "Why don't you start us some coffee while I get the fryers going? The pre-packed filters are in the drawer under the coffeemakers."

"Sounds good. Where should I put my coat?" He unzipped it.

"I'll take it and put it in the office."

James shrugged out of it, then handed it to her. She headed for her office while he walked through the swinging door to the dining room. After stowing their coats, she turned on the fryers to heat them up, then grabbed what she needed to mix up pancake and waffle batter.

"Coffee's brewing. What do you want me to do now?"

"Check the condiment bottles and napkin dispensers. I didn't fill anything before I left yesterday. Once you do that, flip the sign to open and unlock the front door."

He nodded and went back through the swinging door. Sara glanced at the clock, then looked over her ingredients, trying to decide how much batter to make. She didn't want to make too much, or she'd just have to throw it away. Picking up a measuring cup, she went with a quarter of her normal batch. She could always make more if she needed it.

Sara hummed to herself as she worked. Early mornings in

the diner before anyone else arrived were soothing. She liked the quiet and the peace the methodical process of cooking brought her. God knew she needed it today. Waking up to James so close to her—close enough she could smell his scent despite the clean linens he was cocooned in—had awakened more than just her brain. She should have left him at home so she could gain some distance from the feelings he inspired. Reminding herself he was only in town for a short time and that he and his brothers ran roughshod over Daisy for years wasn't helping anymore.

She cracked eggs in a bowl and whisked them faster than usual as her thoughts lingered on the man in the dining room. Why did he have to be so damn handsome? And funny? Despite telling herself she would just tolerate his presence in her home, she'd actually enjoyed their evening together.

That half-smile of his that quirked his mouth when he had a good hand at cards filtered into her mind. Sara groaned and shoved it back out.

Enough!

Pushing James and his quirky smile and deep blue eyes out of her head, she focused on prepping breakfast. She doubted her customers would accept the pancakes were salty or there were eggshells in their waffles because she wasn't paying attention.

∼

The echo of voices filled the diner as James wove through the tables, carrying a tray of dirty dishes. He pushed through the swinging door to the kitchen and deposited them at the dishwashing station.

"Order up!"

He spun on his heel at the sound of Sara's voice, going back to the dining room to get the order from the window.

Swiping at the sweat on his forehead with the arm of his shirt, he piled the plates on his now empty tray and walked back into the dining room. He glanced at the ticket, then at the tables, counting from the door to make sure he got the right one. After he confused three orders, he started writing table numbers on the order tickets. It had helped tremendously.

"Okay, one rancher's platter, one farmyard burger with onion rings, and one chicken-fried steak platter." He set the plates down in front of the three men. "Anything else I can get you?"

They shook their heads.

"Holler at me if there is." He headed for the next table, a man eating alone. "Eight-ounce sirloin, rare, with broccoli and mashed potatoes."

The man glanced up and nodded. James set the plate down, then paused, studying the guy. He looked like something the cat dragged in after a night on the prowl.

"Can I get you anything else?"

"Yeah, some A-1 sauce."

"It should be—" James paused as he looked at the condiment caddy against the wall. It had ketchup, salt, and pepper, but no A-1. "Sorry about that. I'll get you some." He took a step toward the counter.

"Where's Sara?"

James turned back. "Cooking. She's short-staffed today because of the weather."

"You her boyfriend?"

Suspicions rising, James straightened to his full height. "And if I am?"

The man shrugged. "Just asking."

"Either way, it's none of your business. I'll be right back with your sauce." Giving the man a hard look, he spun around, weaving through the tables to take a bottle off the counter. Several new customers on bar stools looked at him.

"Be right with you." He hurried back to the man's table, sitting the bottle by his plate. "You need anything else?"

The guy shook his head. "Nope." He looked up from slicing his steak, his watery blue eyes surprisingly keen for his appearance.

James studied his face for a moment, making a mental note to keep an eye on the man, then nodded. "Holler if you do." Not waiting for a response, he walked back to the counter. As he rounded the corner, he glanced back. The guy had poured A-1 onto his plate and dipped a forkful of bloody meat into it before slipping the bite into his mouth. He stared straight ahead as he chewed.

A frown creased James's forehead. That guy was a little off his rocker. And it bothered him he seemed so curious about Sara's life. He needed to remember to ask her about him later. Make sure she knew the guy was asking personal questions about her.

With a last glance at the stranger, James pasted a smile on his face and turned to the first of the new customers. "Hello. What can I get for you today?"

It was another hour before he paused to take a breath. He swiped sweat from his forehead onto his shoulder again and leaned on the counter. When Sara dragged him here, he really hadn't expected for the diner to be very busy. Boy, was he wrong. It seemed the snow brought in everyone who could get out of their driveways. They started to trickle in around ten. By noon, every table was occupied, and it stayed that way until after one.

Now that there was a lull, though, he needed a drink. Moving to the drink station, he poured himself a glass of water and gulped it down. The kitchen door swung open and Sara walked out holding two plates.

"Lunch." She set the plates on the counter and pushed one toward him. "Turkey bacon club."

"Yum. Thanks." He set his glass down and slid the plate closer. His mouth watered as he closed a hand around half of the sandwich. He didn't realize how hungry he was until now. All that had registered was his thirst.

"Sure. Thanks for helping. You're a good worker." She bit into her sandwich.

He rolled his eyes, swallowing the food in his mouth. "Like you gave me a choice this morning."

She smiled. "True. But you didn't have to work so hard."

His brow furrowed. "Would things have gotten done if I didn't?"

"Well, no."

"Exactly." He popped a potato chip into his mouth. "You needed me. Admit it, Shark." His mouth quirked.

It was Sara's turn to roll her eyes. "Cocky bastard. And really? You were serious about that nickname?" She shook her head as he grinned. "I still can't regret bringing you, though. You saved my ass today."

His eyes strayed to her butt, and a wicked smile crossed his face. Sara's cheeks heated. "Stop staring at my butt."

He grinned and shrugged. "It's a nice butt." He took another bite.

Her cheeks heated further. She ignored him and ate more of her food.

"So, what happens now?"

"We restock the stuff on the tables and tidy-up in back. I made a mess."

"I bet. In Chicago, people stay home when it snows."

"Yeah, well, here, most people don't have that luxury. A lot of the people who were here are ranch hands or forestry workers. I see most of them on a regular basis."

"Really? So you know everyone who comes in?"

She nodded. "It's a small town."

"Hmm. So, who was the guy here about an hour ago? He sat over there and ordered a rare steak."

"Dark hair and blue eyes?"

James nodded.

"Billy Jeffries. Why do you ask?"

"I don't know. There was something about him. He seemed really interested in you. Asked where you were, then if I was your boyfriend."

She shrugged. "I agree he's a little strange, but he's always been nice."

"Just do me a favor and be careful around him. I've been around enough aberrant personalities to recognize weirdness. And he was definitely weird."

"I'm sure he's fine."

"Just promise."

Sara huffed. "Fine. I promise."

"Good." He polished off the last of his sandwich. "I'm going to start on the tables. I'll leave your cooking mess to you."

She laughed. "Okay."

Grinning, he sauntered past her to take his plate to the dishwasher.

Nine

Sara shook her head as she watched James try to get through the door from the garage with all his packages. During their lull this afternoon, he ran to a store downtown to get more clothes. All his were in his suitcase at the Stone Creek, and he didn't want to spend another day in the same clothes. She couldn't blame him. She wouldn't want to, either.

"Did you really need all that? It'll probably be tomorrow when they clear the road to the ranch. You didn't need to buy out the store."

He shrugged and dumped his load on the bar. "My jog down the mountain showed me I'm under prepared for the weather here. I bought some underlayers too." He dug into a bag. "And mittens."

She laughed and took off her coat. "Good. Did you buy wool socks?"

James nodded. "And some thermal shirts."

"Well, why don't you go change while I build a fire? There's enough water pressure for you to wash up from the bathroom sink. Albeit, the water's cold."

"That's fine. I just want to get the grime off."

"Wash cloths are in the linen closet in the bathroom."

He pulled a few items from the sacks. "I'll be back in a few."

Sara watched him go, trying not to stare at his butt as it flexed under his jeans, failing miserably. She growled at herself and stomped into the living room.

She didn't want to like the man. He might not have told Daisy how to dress or who to date, but he never spoke up, either, and defended her to their brothers. And he was a cocky bastard. So sure of himself and his appeal to women.

But he was nice. He'd jumped in when she needed him, doing the job beyond her expectations without complaint. His concern for her when he got a creeper vibe from Billy Jeffries was unexpected. Why couldn't he be an asshole who only thought about himself? It would be much easier to resist that smile and that body if he were.

Huffing, she laid kindling in the fire grate and lit it. She needed to stop giving thoughts of him any brain power. He'd be gone soon, and she'd be back to her normal life. One that didn't include her friend's handsome as sin brother.

The fire crackled as the kindling burned. Sara picked up several logs and laid them over the fire, hugging her arms around herself. She wished she hadn't removed her coat. Spying the blankets they piled on the couch that morning, she grabbed one and wrapped it around herself, settling in front of the flames.

"I feel more human now."

She glanced back at the sound of James's voice and nearly swallowed her tongue. He'd changed, all right. Into a muscle-hugging, forest green thermal henley over a white t-shirt and gray sweats that highlighted everything he had beneath.

"Um," she cleared her throat and looked away. "Good."

He snagged another blanket and sat down next to her,

wrapping it around his shoulders. "So, what's on the agenda tonight? More cards?"

Unbidden, Sara smiled. As much as she enjoyed kicking his sexy butt at Uno, she had other ideas for tonight. "No. Hang on." She stood, taking her blanket with her, and went to the kitchen where she left her big tote bag of a purse, then returned to the living room. "After your writing breakthrough last night, I decided to take my laptop to work with us today." She sat down and took it from her bag. "I charged it in my office so you could work on your book."

His eyes widened. "You did?" He took the laptop from her. "You didn't have to do that."

"I know. But you are here to write. Being stuck at my house without your computer shouldn't prevent you from doing that."

"I don't know what to say."

Sara giggled. "You don't have to say anything. It's just a laptop."

He stared at her a moment longer. Without warning, he grabbed the edges of her blanket and yanked her forward, pressing his lips to hers.

Sara let out an involuntary squeak before her body took over, and she sank into him. He groaned and edged closer, opening his mouth over hers. Even with her mind screaming at her they shouldn't do this, her body didn't care. Her mouth parted beneath his to let him in. At the first touch of his tongue to hers, she melted. Heat suffused her, and every bone in her body turned to liquid.

Their blankets fell away as James shifted to bring her closer. Her hands landed on his chest to curl into the soft fabric of his shirt. She felt his muscles shift beneath her knuckles, and the urge to ruck up his shirt to touch them hit her hard. Hard enough to jolt her back to her senses. She pushed away, breathing hard. "What the hell was that?"

A naughty smile tilted his mouth. "A thank you?"

She rolled her eyes and tucked herself back into her blanket. "The words would have sufficed."

He shrugged. "Wouldn't have been half as fun." His half-smile bloomed to cover his face. Those blue eyes crinkled at the corners and sparkled in the firelight.

Sara squashed the answering smile trying to break free. "Write your book." She got to her feet. "I'm going to read one."

The smile broke free as she walked away to his laugh.

Ten

James looked up at the sound of the cowbell to see his sister and brother-in-law walk into the diner. Daisy's eyes widened as she spotted him. He could only imagine what was going through her head.

"Hey, guys. Finally plowed out, I see."

"And we found your car." Asa stepped up to the counter where James was busy pouring drinks for table six. "Jasper and I towed it back to the ranch before Daisy and I came down to fetch you."

"Oh." A frown dipped James's brow. "I wish you'd have called first. I can't leave yet."

"What do you mean?" Daisy leaned against the counter.

He gestured at the busy restaurant. "It's too busy for me to leave just yet. I probably won't be ready until after we close tonight."

Daisy blinked at him. "We?"

James nodded and set the last soda on his tray, then picked it up. "Sara's short-handed. I can't leave." He walked out from behind the counter. "If you want lunch, I suggest you grab any open seats you can find before someone else does." The bell sounded again as more people entered. He sauntered away, grinning at the wide-eyed look on Daisy's face.

When he turned around, they were seated at the counter, looking at menus. He stopped to take a couple of orders, then went to the window to pass the slips to Sara before turning to his sister. "Decided to stay for lunch, huh?"

"Mostly to figure out who you are and what you did with my brother."

James rolled his eyes, slightly annoyed. "I'm not an ogre, Dais. Helping Sara is the least I can do after she took me in. And I'm so glad you were concerned about me. It's nice to know you care." Sarcasm dripped off his words.

Her mouth flattened. "I am glad you're okay. Next time you decide to be so pig-headed, I'll be sure to stop you."

"Yeah, well, next time, I'll probably listen. I'm sorry I didn't."

"Order up!"

He glanced back at Sara's shout. "I'll be back to take your orders." James spun back to the window and gathered the plates onto a tray, walking past Daisy and Asa. He made a quick trip through the dining room to deliver the food, then pick up dirty dishes before disappearing into the back.

"Was that Daisy I saw out there?" Sara looked over from her place at the grill.

James deposited the dishes at the dishwashing station and glanced back. "Yeah. The road to the ranch is clear. Asa and Jasper already got my car from the ditch. She said they're here to get me."

"Oh. Well, um, thanks for the help yesterday and today."

He smiled. "Who said I'm leaving?"

She frowned. "But your sister—"

"Is going to eat lunch and go home. I'll join her there after we close."

"Oh." Her frowned turned curious. "How will you get there?"

He paused on his way to the door. A slow smile spread over his face. "Can I bum a ride?"

Sara laughed, and he chuckled.

"I suppose it's the least I can do for all the help you've been."

"Good. Thanks."

She smiled. "Get back to work, slacker."

He barked a laugh and pushed through the door. His eyes landed on Daisy. "You guys decide what you want?"

"Yeah. But first, I want to know what happened in the last two days. She was ready to throttle you when I mentioned you were here. Now you two are laughing and joking?"

He shrugged, smiling. "What can I say? She can't resist me."

Daisy rolled her eyes. Asa snorted.

"That'll be the day." Daisy lifted her menu, staring at it. "It might be lunchtime, but I want an omelet." She paused and looked at him. "Wait. You're not doing the cooking, are you?"

"I might make an exception for you, Sis." He gave her a wicked grin.

She wrinkled her nose. "Please don't."

His smile widened. "Relax. Sara won't let me near the grill."

"Smart woman."

"Hey, I can cook. I've lived on my own my entire adult life."

It was Daisy's turn to snort. "You lived off cafeteria food and ramen while you were in college. After that, you ate out."

"I can make the basics. Eggs count as a basic."

"Still, I'd rather have Sara's."

He pouted, putting a hand over his heart. "You wound me." James knew he was laying it on a bit thick, but she was fun to tease. And for the first time in a long time, she wasn't getting mad at him when he did it. He called it progress. He had a lot to make up for.

"Oh, whatever. I want ham, cheese, peppers, and onions in it, please."

James shook his head, grinning. He took his order pad and pen from his apron pocket and wrote down her order. "What about you, Asa?"

"Breakfast for lunch sounds good. I'll take a stack of pancakes, bacon, and some scrambled eggs."

"Drinks?"

"Coffee's fine," Daisy said.

"Same." Asa put his menu back in the holder in front of them.

He finished scribbling their order on the notepad and tore off the sheet, hanging it with the others in the window. Sara set two more plates on the ledge and took the ticket for them down to set with the plates.

"That one's ready."

"Okay, thanks." He loaded up a tray and headed for the tables, ignoring his sister's curious stare.

∽

Sara glanced up as the kitchen door swung open again. She expected to see James, but it was Daisy.

"Hey, girl." She smiled at her friend. "Glad to see you made it off the mountain."

"Apparently not soon enough. I've walked into a scene from *Invasion of the Body Snatchers*."

"Huh?" Sara flipped a burger. "What are you talking about?"

"What am I—?" Daisy propped a hand on her hip. "Have you seen Penny out there?"

Sara rolled her eyes at the *Big Bang Theory* reference and pointed her spatula at Daisy. "Penny sucked at waitressing. James doesn't. You'd be better off comparing him to Bernadette."

"Semantics. My point is he's never worked in the food industry, even in college. He worked in the law library."

"I don't know what to tell you." She plated the burger. "He jumped in when I asked him to help and has been doing great." She added fries to the plate and set it in the window under the heat lights. "I don't know what I'd have done without him. Especially yesterday. I had him and the dishwasher. Today, at least, I have a second server."

Daisy shook her head. "You sure he didn't hit his head when he ran off the road?"

Sara giggled. "Yes. He was just cold."

"And what's with you?"

"Me?" She added cheese to several hamburger patties, keeping her gaze from connecting with Daisy's.

"Yes, you. When you found out he was here, you were ready to send him packing for me. Now you're all buddy-buddy. I thought for sure you'd murder him before he returned to the Stone Creek."

Sara chanced a glance at her friend. Daisy narrowed her eyes.

"What happened to make you change your tune?"

"Nothing." She shrugged and looked away. "I just got to know him. He's not that bad."

Silence met her words. She chanced another look back.

Daisy's eyes went wide. "Oh my God, you like him!"

"What? No!" Sara mentally cursed. That was probably too much protesting to be believable. She should have laughed it off.

"Liar."

Sara's shoulders slumped. "Okay, so maybe I think he's attractive. And not a total asshat. But that doesn't mean anything. He'll be gone in a week."

"Unless he decides to stay."

A fierce frown creased Sara's forehead. "What do you mean?"

Grinning, Daisy crossed her arms. "He doesn't have a job to get back to. What's stopping him from staying here to finish his book?"

Sara's eyes grew round. "No. He can't stay. He needs to go back to Chicago. Where he lives." She'd already kissed him once. What would she do if he stuck around? Did she want a fling? Could she do casual sex? The last time that happened, she was in college. Since then, well, she found other ways to find release. But sex was where they were headed if he kept kissing her the way he did last night.

Daisy giggled. "Oh, this is going to be fun."

"No, there's no fun to be had. He's leaving and I'm staying, where I will continue to live my boring life."

"You keep telling yourself that." She shook a finger at Sara. "I did the same thing when Asa came home. Told myself nothing would ever happen. That I didn't want a relationship."

"Yes, but he wasn't going anywhere. James is leaving. Even if he stays longer than the end of next week, he'll still leave."

"Unless he has a reason to stay." Daisy shrugged, a wicked smile forming on her face. "Anyway, I just came to see why you hadn't killed him yet. Now I know. I'm going back out with my husband."

Sara stared at her, mouth agape.

Daisy pointed to the grill as she backed toward the door. "I think your burgers are burning."

"What?" Sara spun around to see smoke rising from the cooking meat. "Shit!"

Eleven

Sunshine glinted off the sea of white in the yard outside James's bedroom window at Daisy's. He was supposed to be writing, but he couldn't concentrate. All he kept seeing was Sara's pretty face when she dropped him off at the ranch last night after the diner closed. She'd looked tired. He tried to get her to stay here, where they had electricity thanks to the powerful generators hard-wired into the ranch buildings, but she just shook her head and said she'd be fine at home. He could have pushed, but truthfully, he needed a break from her—from the feelings she provoked. Several times yesterday, he had to stop himself from leaning in to kiss her just because he wanted to.

In the light of day, though, he couldn't help but wonder how she fared last night and how things were going today. She was still short a cook. He just hoped her other server made it into work.

James twisted his neck and sighed. He needed to get back to work and stop daydreaming. Adjusting the laptop propped over his thighs, he looked at the screen. The cursor blinked at him, taunting him to write. Sara's face popped into his head again.

With a curse, he closed the lid and stood, tossing the computer onto the bed. This was ridiculous. He'd do better writing once he satisfied himself she wasn't running herself ragged.

His feet thumped softly on the stairs as he made his way down to find his boots and coat. Thankfully, his rental car didn't have too much damage. He'd already called the rental company and his insurance. The car was still driveable, so the rental agency told him to hang on to it until his return flight at the end of the week.

He passed the living room on his way to the kitchen. Daisy glanced over from dusting a bookshelf. "Hi. You come up for air finally?"

"Something like that." He paused, frowning, as he spotted the duster in her hand. "You need help with anything?"

She shook her head. "It's not laundry day, so no." She pointed the feathered wand at him. "Stop procrastinating."

"I'm not. I'm going to town. I'll be back later." He spun on his heel and headed for the mudroom off the kitchen.

"What?"

James heard her follow him, but didn't stop. He bent down and picked up a boot, leaning against the wall to shove his foot inside. A glance at his sister showed him the knowing smile on her face.

"Feeling peckish?"

"No."

"Liar."

He pulled his other boot on, then crouched to tie them. "I'm just going to check on her, is all."

"Right. Because she hasn't been running that diner for years all by herself."

"Well," he shrugged into his coat, "is she normally down to less than a handful of employees?"

Daisy's mouth flattened and her brow wrinkled. "Maybe I should go with you."

"Oh, no. Asa would kill me if I took you there and you worked. I'm supposed to be here taking some of your workload away, not adding to it."

She chuckled. "So you're abandoning me?"

"I can stay—"

"Pfft, no. I told you when you got here, I don't really need help. Carrying anything heavy or bulky is really it anymore. I'm just going to finish dusting, then make some snacks for the hands, maybe prep a bit for Thanksgiving. No heavy lifting required." She made a shooing motion. "Go check on Sara."

James smiled and zipped his coat, then leaned in to peck his sister's cheek. "I'll see you later."

She smiled. "Be careful."

He put his gloves on and headed for the door. "Tell that to the elk." Twisting the knob, he smiled at her and let himself out.

Icy wind blasted him, swirling the snow to whip it into his face like millions of tiny needles. A shiver ripped down his spine. He wasn't really cold, but his body remembered the other day. If he ever got caught out in the snow like that again, it would be too soon. He fumbled with the key fob in his pocket, his thick gloves getting in the way, but finally pressed the unlock button. Yanking on the door handle, he got into his car. James pushed the button to start it and cranked up the heat.

Once the fog on the windshield disappeared, he put the car in gear and steered the vehicle down the driveway. He was cautious on the way into town, not wanting a repeat of the other day, and took the curves much slower than normal. No elk were going to surprise him again. Forty-five minutes after he left the ranch, he pulled into a parking spot at Sarafina's and shut off the engine.

He glanced around as he walked toward the door. The parking lot was full. Only a couple of spots remained.

The bell over the door tinkled as he walked inside. Noise greeted him. As he tugged off his gloves, he looked over the dining room to see a lone server wandering through the tables. It was a different person from yesterday.

James pushed through the kitchen door and turned to see Sara at the grill. "Why didn't you call me? Or the woman who worked yesterday?"

She looked over, surprise on her face. "Hey. What are you doing here?"

"Saving your ass again. Answer my question."

She rolled her eyes. "Rachel's son caught that flu that's going around. She called me last night after I got home to tell me he was running a fever."

"Okay. So, why didn't you call me?"

"Why would I?" She cracked two eggs into a bowl and whisked them with a fork. "You're here to help Daisy and write your book, not wait tables for me."

"Well, I'm amending my reasons for being here. I'm your new waiter." He unzipped his coat and shrugged out of it.

Her eyes, which were on his chest, snapped to his face. "What? No, I don't need another waiter. We're doing fine."

James rolled his eyes. "Sure you are. That girl out there looks like she's run a marathon." He walked toward her and held out a hand. "Keys."

Sara poured the eggs on the grill. "Why?"

"So I can put my coat in your office. Keys."

She held his gaze. "You're not leaving, are you?"

"Nope."

Heaving a sigh, she dug into her apron and produced a set of keys, dropping them into his palm.

"Thank you." He spun on his heel and headed for her office. Inside, he hung his jacket on the coat rack she had in the corner, then plucked an apron off the pile and tied it around his waist. After a quick stop in the storage room for an order pad and pen, he headed out front to help wait tables.

"You don't know how happy I am to see you." The young woman leaned against the counter and blew her blonde bangs out of her face. "I'm Leslie."

"James." He smiled. "I think I can imagine. Where do you want me?"

"Can you handle the counter and the front row of tables?"

"Sure."

"Tables two and six are new. I don't know about the counter people. There have been some coming in for to-go orders."

"I'll go down the line."

"Order up!"

Leslie hurried around him to take the plates. James turned to the counter patrons and asked each one if they'd ordered. Once he had that area square, he wandered out to the front row of tables to take orders.

The lunch rush passed in a blur. James didn't look at the clock until just after two when the last customer left the diner. Blowing out a breath, he poured himself a glass of water and chugged it.

"That was brutal." Leslie collapsed onto a bar stool. "Pour me one of those, would you?"

He refilled his glass and poured her one. "Is it always like that?"

"Most days, yes. But we usually have more help. Becky quit to move to Billings. Melody's out with the flu, Rachel's out because her little boy has it too, and the only other help Sara has are high school kids who can only work evenings and weekends. Luckily, there's two of them coming in just over an hour. Once they get here, I'm going home and not moving the rest of the night."

A crash in the kitchen drew James's attention before he could reply. He and Leslie shared an alarmed look, before they spun toward the kitchen.

"What happened?" He pushed through the door, Leslie on his heels, to see Sara bending over to pick up shards of ceramic.

"I dropped a plate. It was too close to the edge of the table, and I hit it with my elbow."

James crouched in front of her. He could hear the weariness in her voice. "Why don't you go sit down in your office for a few minutes? I'll clean this up." She had to be exhausted. At least he and Leslie were away from the heat of the grill. He could see the sweat beaded on Sara's temples and the flush to her cheeks.

"It's fine. It'll only take me a minute."

"Exactly." He took the plate shards from her and set them on the floor before pulling her to her feet. "Come on."

"What? No, James. I have work to do." She tugged against his hold.

"That can wait a few minutes while you sit down and get something to drink." He tightened his grip and led her toward the office. Taking her keys from his apron, he held on to her with one hand in case she bolted.

With a quick twist of his wrist, he unlocked the door and pulled her inside, pushing her into the desk chair. She huffed up at him.

"Stay." He pointed a finger at her.

"I'm not a dog, James."

"Never said you were. Stay put, okay? I'll have Leslie

bring you some water while I clean up the broken plate." He didn't wait for her to answer—didn't want to give her a chance to protest further. She'd just be blowing hot air. Leaving the office, he spotted Leslie by the grill with the broom.

"I was going to do that."

She smiled. "I know. But you were busy convincing the boss she needed to take a break." She crouched and swept the debris into the dustpan.

"I'll get her a drink, then. Thanks."

"Not a problem."

James walked into the dining room and headed for the pop machine, filling a glass with water. He snagged a piece of cherry pie from the cooler under the counter and headed back to the office. Sara had turned and now stared at her computer screen.

Annoyance made him frown. He set the pie plate and water down on the desk, then grasped the arm of her chair and spun her towards him. "You're supposed to be resting."

She arched a brow, looking just as annoyed. "I'm still sitting, aren't I?"

"Shark—"

"Stop calling me that."

He pressed lips together and stared down at her. She huffed again, making him smile.

An answering one twitched her lips. "Stop. I'm mad at you." She leaned an elbow on the chair arm and covered her mouth.

"Sure you are. Eat your pie."

A giggle slid past her lips. "I can't."

He frowned and straightened. "Why not?"

"You forgot the fork."

James sighed and left the office, walking to the dishwasher and taking a clean fork from the rack of silverware Jerry just ran. He returned to her side, holding out the utensil as he bowed low. "Madam."

Sara giggled again and took the fork. "Thank you, good sir."

He plopped into the chair snug against the side of her desk, groaning as the weight left his feet. "I should have worn different shoes."

"I'd say you should have stayed home and worked on your book, but I'd be lying if I said I wasn't thankful you showed up."

"You need more help."

She shrugged and picked up her pie plate. "I normally don't have any issues. And it's not like I'm a big company that can rotate workers to cover when I have multiple people out sick. We'll get by. We always do." She lifted a bite of the pie. "You're a big part of that this time." The bite disappeared between her lips.

James looked away, muscles tense, as that fork slid past her pretty lips. His dirty mind went straight to what else he'd like to see her wrap those lips around.

He cleared his throat and fought to find a distraction. "So, what was so important on your computer you couldn't even take a five-minute break?" He pointed at her screen.

She looked over her shoulder, fork hanging from her mouth. "Oh, I was putting in a last-minute order for Thursday's dinner."

"Thursday?" He frowned. "That's Thanksgiving. Aren't you closed?"

"Yes, but I'm in charge of my church's Thanksgiving soup kitchen that day. I always donate food and my time." Her nose scrunched. "Unfortunately, this year, I also got talked into spearheading the whole thing. This morning, the lady who runs the church's food bank emailed me the final number of people they expect to attend, and I realized I didn't have enough food."

"Is that how you always spend Thanksgiving?"

"Mostly. I spend Christmas with my parents, either here or down in New Mexico. This year, I'm going there. We rotate every other year."

"So, no one ever cooks for you on Thanksgiving?"

She shook her head and ate another bite of pie.

James didn't like that. This woman worked hard all day every day and deserved a break as well as a chance to enjoy the holiday. "What time is this shindig on Thursday?"

"Lunch-ish. We start serving at eleven, and it goes until we run out of food."

"Which is?"

Sara shrugged. "Two or so, usually. I'm not sure this year with the crowd they're expecting. The mine closures hit this area hard, so there are more people out of work."

"Well, regardless of what time you're done, why don't you come out to the ranch afterward? Daisy's already started prepping. She'll make enough to feed a small army, so I know she wouldn't mind one more."

"You sure about that? Remember what happened the last time one of you invited someone over to dinner without consulting her first?"

James grinned. "Well, yeah, but you're not a tiny, bulldog-looking man with bad manners. You're her friend. And you know damn well she'd invite you over herself if she knew you would be alone."

She ate another bite of pie and tried to look innocent.

He shook his head. "Why don't you want to come?"

"I don't know. I guess I'm just used to being alone. I've done the soup kitchen every year since my parents moved away. It's always been enough for me, and I enjoy it."

"Well, how about this year, you try something new?"

She shot him a look from the side of her eye. "I'll think about it, okay?" Putting her plate down, she picked up her water glass and took a hearty drink.

James sat back in his chair and crossed his arms. "Good. In the meantime, where do I sign up for this thing?"

Sara choked on her water, sputtering it down her front. "What?"

"Your Thanksgiving meal at the church. How do I sign up to help serve?"

"Why?" She found a clean bar towel and dabbed at her face and shirt.

"Because I want to help."

"Again, why?" She paused in drying herself off to give him a droll look. "You don't know anyone in town. You don't even live here. Why would you want to help our community?"

James did his best to keep his expression clear. She would have to ask him that. Honestly, the words just popped out before he had a chance to really think about them. But if he did, he knew his answer would be because of the woman sitting next to him. "Look, I just do, okay? Can we drop it?"

A grin spread over her face, and James groaned.

"No. No, we cannot." She crossed her arms and her legs. "Tell me, James O'Malley. Why do you want to help feed the hungry with me?"

"I don't care what you say; I'm calling you Shark whenever I feel like it. Once you sink your teeth into something, you just don't let go, do you?" He stood. "You know what? Forget I asked." In one long stride, he was at the door.

"Wait!" Her small hands grabbed his arm as he was about to step through the doorway. "I'm sorry. I won't ask again. You're more than welcome to help out."

James's arm burned where she touched him. The heat raced a path up to his neck and down his spine. He gave her a curt nod, incapable of anything more if he wanted to keep his composure and not yank her out of that chair and kiss her again. "Okay. Text me the information. I need to get back out there and see if Leslie needs any help." He hooked a thumb toward the dining room.

She let him go and rose. "Yeah. I should clean the grill while it's quiet."

With another nod, he spun around and hightailed it back to the dining room and away from temptation.

Twelve

Groaning, Sara arched her back and pressed her fist into her lower spine. When she got home, she was sinking into the bathtub. Her power came back on this morning, and she was taking full advantage of it.

She reached forward and turned off her monitor, done with the daily expense report, and pushed back from her desk. As she stood, her gaze landed on James's coat still draped over the guest chair in her office. She'd forgotten he was still here. Picking up his coat, she left her office and locked it.

"James?" Sara wandered through the kitchen and pushed open the door to the dining room. He sat at a table, a glass of water in front of him as he typed into his phone.

"Hey." He glanced up as she came through the door.

"Hey yourself. What are you still doing here?"

"Waiting on you to finish."

She stopped in front of him. "Why?"

He shrugged and stood, taking his coat from her. "Didn't want you to be here alone, so I waited. I did some writing while you finished up."

Sara wasn't sure why he would do that, but in the end, it

was his time he was burning, not hers, so it didn't bother her. The only thing that did was the warm fuzzy feeling brought on by his actions. She liked that he waited for her, but she didn't want to like it. "Well, I'm ready to go. Are you?"

"Yes." He put his coat on and zipped it, tucking his phone in his pocket. "Lead the way." He picked up his glass and followed her back through the kitchen, leaving it at the dishwashing station. They exited the building.

"Where did you park?" she asked, her eyes roving the empty lot.

"Way back there." He pointed to the back corner.

She glanced over to see his white SUV tucked into a spot on the far side of the parking area under a tree. "Okay, well, thanks again for helping out today. I appreciate it."

"Of course. I'll be here tomorrow, too, and every day after that you need me until I have to go back to Chicago."

She bit the corner of her bottom lip. "James—"

He laid a finger over her lips. "No arguing. You need help. I have time."

Sara's lips tingled beneath his finger, and she swallowed against the lump of need forming in her throat. "Okay," she whispered.

"Good."

The smile that bloomed on his face sucked her breath away. Damn, but he was a handsome devil.

But just as quickly as it appeared, it vanished as he glanced around.

"What?"

"Huh?" He looked at her.

"Why are you frowning all of a sudden?"

Those deep blue eyes of his studied her for a moment. "There's a man sitting in a truck over there." He tipped his head to his left. "It looks like the guy from the diner. The one I asked you about."

Sara glanced past his shoulder at the ancient burgundy truck parked near the street light. She could just make out the figure of a man in the driver's seat. "How can you tell? It's dark inside the cab."

"He was leaning forward when I looked over there. Is that truck often out here at night when you leave?"

"I don't know." She shrugged. "I guess I don't pay that much attention."

"You don't pay—" James sighed and pinched the bridge of his nose. "Seriously? Sara, you're a beautiful woman alone after dark and you don't pay attention to your surroundings?"

She glared at him. "It's not like Pine Ridge is a hotbed of rapists and murderers. And I always park right outside the door. It's like ten steps to the driver's seat."

"It doesn't matter. Weirdos are everywhere. They're universal, Shark."

"I told you to stop calling me that."

"You just don't like it because it's true." His mouth quirked.

Sara saw red. Egotistical pig-headed asshat. She was not ruthless like the name implied. So what that she was tenacious? She wasn't mindless. And she'd tired of this argument. "Bite me, James O'Malley." She spun around, intending to get in her car, but he caught her hand and turned her back.

"Oomph!" She landed against his hard chest with a thump. Sara raised a finger and looked up, intending to give him a piece of her mind, but the heated smile on his face stopped her.

"Gladly." He leaned down, stopping millimeters from her lips.

The fine hairs on Sara's neck raised. Her body tingled where it contacted his. She felt his breath fan over her face. Pulling back a fraction, she looked into his eyes. An answering heat filled their blue depths. Unable to resist his pull, she closed the distance and sealed her mouth to his.

True to his word, he nipped at her bottom lip. She moaned and kissed him harder. Her fingers speared through his hair; the strands were cool from the chilly air.

His mouth left hers to trail along her jaw and behind her ear. Sara clutched his shoulders as he scrambled her brain. Her breath puffed white in the frigid night, but she barely noticed the cold. James heated her body from the inside out.

An engine starting, then accelerating as it drove away, brought her back to earth. She broke away, still holding his shoulders as she stared up into his eyes. His chest heaved against hers as he held her gaze.

"Why do you make me forget I'm mad at you?"

"Talent." He let her go, his smile absent.

Sara shivered as she thought about what particular talents he might have that could make her forget a whole lot more than why she was upset.

"You're cold," he said, misinterpreting her tremor. He turned her toward her car. "Come on. It's late anyway, so you should get going. We both should."

"Yeah." She inhaled a deep lungful of the chilly air, hoping it helped to cool her blood and her thoughts. Thrusting a hand in her coat pocket, she pushed the button on her key fob to unlock the car, then pulled on the handle.

"What time do you want me here tomorrow?" James laid a hand over the top of the door as she stood in the opening.

Never. Not if she stood a chance of resisting him. But she knew he'd ignore her and show up anyway. "Depends on how early you want to get up and if Daisy needs you. The breakfast rush starts about six-thirty."

"Okay. I'll ask her what she has planned for tomorrow. If I'm going to be late, I'll call."

"You know—"

"Don't even say it. You won't change my mind." He pointed at the driver's seat. "Get in the car."

Sara huffed. Damn stubborn man. Glaring at him, she sank into the seat and yanked the door closed. Her last glimpse of him was in her rearview mirror as he climbed into his car while she drove out of the parking lot.

Thirteen

"Hey, Rach? Are you good?" Sara poked her head through the kitchen door to the dining room to speak to Rachel, who'd returned to work. She and her husband had swapped out in taking care of their sick son, so neither of them burned through too much sick time.

"Yep. Go run your errands. Les and I will hold down the fort."

"Thanks, I appreciate it. I won't be gone too long."

Rachel waved a hand. "Take your time. It's always slow this time of day."

"Okay. I turned off one side of the grill, so just watch which side you cook on."

The other woman nodded, and Sara ducked back into the kitchen to retrieve her coat and purse from her office. She had a mountain of errands to run for the church's Thanksgiving meal. Several local businesses and organizations called, saying they had donations. Plus, she had to drop off the extra food she ordered.

After loading her SUV with the items delivered that morning, Sara wound her way through town, picking up supplies at several places, then heading for the church. She was going to drop it all off, then head back to the diner for the dinner rush.

The same beat-up truck that was outside the diner the other night when James kissed her was parked on the street next to the church. Unease tingled between her shoulder blades as she turned into the church parking lot. As she parked near the rear entrance, she rolled her eyes at herself. Mr. Big City Man had her believing in the boogeyman. She'd known Billy Jeffries for years. He'd never been anything but polite. Quiet and a little withdrawn, maybe, but always polite. She'd certainly never got any creeper vibes off of him.

Still, it unnerved her a bit that he happened to be where she was. It wasn't a secret she was in charge of the dinner this year, and she didn't know what reason he would have for being at the church; he wasn't a member, and she knew he wasn't homeless or hurting for money—even though he didn't dress the best—so he wouldn't be here for the food bank.

She climbed out of her car, glancing around as she went to the rear of the vehicle to open the back hatch. Hefting a box of disposable plates donated by the employees at the sheriff's department, she headed for the door.

"Dammit." She paused, staring at the doorknob. Her keys were in her pocket. Pressing the box against the door, she leaned into it, holding it there while she rummaged for them. She took them out and found the church key, then pulled the box back from the door to try to unlock it. As she stabbed at the lock, the keys slipped from her hand to drop into the slush at her feet.

"Really?" She sighed and tipped her head back, pleading with a higher power to help her work through her to-do list quickly and efficiently.

"Do you need some help?"

She jumped at the voice behind her and spun around to

see Billy standing there. His shock of silver-streaked dark hair was mussed, like he just woke up, but his eyes were clear.

"Oh, um, I'm good. I just dropped my keys. Thanks, though."

He ignored her and stepped forward, bending down to pick her keys out of the snow. "Which one?"

"It's, um, that one." She nodded at the gold key in his right hand.

Billy inserted it into the lock and opened the door.

"Thank you." She ducked her head and walked inside. When she came back out, he had a load of boxes in his arms and was coming toward her.

"Oh, you didn't have to do that, Mr. Jeffries. I can get it."

"It's no problem. Just point me to where you want me to put this stuff."

"That table there is fine." Sara pointed to the closest of the long tables church volunteers set up for the diners tomorrow.

He set the boxes down without a word, then went back for more. Sara followed him out to help. When she went out for a third load, another car pulled up next to hers. She recognized James behind the wheel.

"Hey, what are you doing here?" She leaned into the car to pull a box of canned yams toward her as he exited his vehicle.

"I was on my way to the diner to help with the dinner shift —Daisy finally sprung me; it was laundry day—and I saw your car." He tipped his chin to the beat-up truck next to her SUV. "What's he doing here?"

"Helping."

"Really."

She ignored his deadpan tone and thrust the box at him. "Yep. And so are you, if you're just going to stand there yapping at me."

His jaw twitched, but he carried it inside. She rolled her eyes as he gave Billy a long look when they crossed paths.

"This is the last of it." She handed Billy a box, then picked up another. "Thank you for all your help."

"Not a problem. I was dropping off my own donation for tomorrow's meal when I saw you."

"Oh? What did you bring?"

"Eggs. My chickens went a little overboard this month."

Sara chuckled. "That's not a bad problem to have."

"No, most definitely not." He set his box on the table with the others. "I should be going." He touched his forehead with two fingers like he was doffing a hat. With a quick glance at James, he headed for the door.

"Thanks again," she called after him. Setting her box down, she turned to James. He stood beside all the boxes and bags they just brought in with his arms crossed and a dark scowl on his face.

"What?"

"Don't 'what' me. I told you he gave me the heebie-jeebies."

She cast a look at him, then started sorting things. The tableware and serving stuff could stay out here, but the food needed to go into the kitchen. "I told him I could handle it, but he insisted."

"Of course he did."

"He was just being nice, James. He said he stopped to donate some eggs and saw me bringing things in. What should I have done? Yelled at him to go away?"

James huffed and dropped his arms. "I just don't like the guy."

"You're paranoid after living in Chicago all your life. Here." She picked up a box and shoved it into his arms. "Take this to the kitchen for me, please."

He glanced into the box, then at the table laden with foodstuffs. "Please tell me you're not cooking all of this by yourself. You'll never sleep tonight."

She laughed and picked up another box. "I have help, but I still don't plan on sleeping much. After the diner closes, I have to come back here to help make some of the sides, then I'll be back before dawn to put turkeys in the ovens and roasters. I'm just glad Cynthia convinced her bible study group to bake all the hams."

"Who's Cynthia?" He followed her into the kitchen, where several women worked.

"The food bank manager."

"How come she's not here to help you unload all this?"

"She's at home, baking pies for tomorrow."

James's eyebrows shot up. "You let someone else bake the pie? Asa says you have the best pie around."

Sara blushed as the women looked up, blatantly listening to their conversation. She smiled and ushered him out of the kitchen. "Watch what you say."

"Huh? Why?"

"Because them's fightin' words, O'Malley. These ladies take their pie seriously. I know I make good pie, but around here, Cynthia's pie queen. She claimed them early on, and I wasn't about to argue. That'll get me running the show again next year too." She picked up another box.

"How did you get it this year?"

"We drew names. I got lucky." She tossed him a saucy smile.

He grinned back. "Right."

Giggling, she took her box to the kitchen. They made several more trips before everything was where it was supposed to be.

"That's everything." She smiled at the women. "I'll be back later. Call if you need something."

A chorus of goodbyes echoed around them as Sara led James from the church.

"How about you ride with me?" he said. "I'm coming back here with you later, anyway."

"You're—I have plenty of help tonight. You can go home. What happened to that book you have to write?"

He waved a hand and steered her toward his car. "I've been working on it every spare moment. It's coming along fine now that I have a solid idea to work with."

"Okay, but I still don't need extra help."

"Sure you do. You're feeding a small army. The more hands, the better, right?" He gave her that roguish grin of his.

She growled, which only made him laugh.

"Do you delight in annoying me?" She put her hands on her hips and glared.

His smile widened. "Well, yeah. You're cute when you're pissed. All baby shark."

"If you start singing that song, I swear I will make you wash dishes by hand all night."

He laughed. "Fine, no song. Get in the car."

She stood there, still glaring.

"Please?" His eyebrows went up with his inflection.

A smile threatened at the boyish quality to his expression, and she rolled her lips in, holding it back, then huffed. "Fine." She tugged on the passenger door handle and got in. He climbed in beside her, then cranked the engine and drove out of the lot.

Sara stared out the window at the houses they passed, doing her best to ignore the scent of him invading the space. The subtle woodsy aroma mixed with man had her body tingling in all the right places. She wanted to lean into him and bury her nose in his neck to get a better whiff. As soon as he parked the car, she was out the door and headed inside to get away from the intoxicating scent before she did just that.

Luckily, the restaurant was already busy. After taking off their coats and donning aprons, they went their separate ways, and she was able to calm her raging hormones. Before she knew it, it was going on seven o'clock. She sent the two high-schoolers home when the dining room cleared out, then locked the door. Her dishwasher, Jerry, was almost finished with the last of the dishes, then he was leaving too. Then it would just be her and James.

She glanced through the order window at the man in question. A cute wrinkle formed between his brows as he concentrated on filling ketchup bottles. Sara shook her head at herself and went back to cleaning. Ogling him wouldn't get her work done. She wanted to attempt to sleep at least a few hours tonight.

Scowling, she poured degreaser on the grill and scrubbed it with steel wool, then wiped it clean.

James came through the door. "Dining room is good to go, and I ran the register receipts." He held up a zippered bank pouch. "Do you need me to do anything in here?"

"No." She pulled off her disposable gloves and tossed them in the trash. "I just finished. Let me wash my hands and we can go." She walked over to the sink and squeezed a glob of soap into her palm. He came up next to her, setting the pouch on the shelf above the sink, and did the same. Sara bit back a moan. Even through the odor of fried food, she could smell his scent.

She rinsed her hands and moved away to get a towel. Why didn't she put her foot down about him helping her at the church tonight? The next few hours would be torture. Maybe she could set him up on the opposite side of the kitchen. At least then she wouldn't be able to smell him. Though she'd still be able to see him, and that was just as bad. She glanced back as she headed for her office to get their coats. He finished drying his hands and tossed the towel in the hamper, forearms flexing below his pushed-up shirtsleeves. Memories assailed her of him coming out of the bathroom after his shower that day she found him half-frozen, and she bit back a moan.

Disgusted with herself, she shoved the thoughts away and picked up her coat, thrusting her arms into it. She took her purse from the desk drawer and turned to leave, rocking to a halt at the sight of James in the doorway.

"What?"

He frowned. "What do you mean, what?"

"Why are you standing there staring at me?"

"I'm not. I was waiting for you to move or hand me my coat." He pointed to the black jacket still draped over the chair next to her.

"Oh." She reached for it and held it out, not wanting him anywhere near her at the moment. She was too tired to fight her attraction to him right now.

"Thanks." He eyed her with suspicion, but took it, passing her the bank pouch, then put the coat on and stepped back.

Sara locked the pouch in her safe, then breezed past him to the back door. She put her hand in her coat pocket, pressing the button to unlock her car, only to realize they drove his. Gritting her teeth, she looked back as he stepped outside, testing the door once it closed to make sure it was locked.

The car beeped as he unlocked it, and she yanked the handle, climbing inside.

"Okay, why are you pissed?" He turned to her as he settled into his seat.

"What? I'm not pissed."

"Sure. And I'm the pope." He started the car. "We both know that's not true, so how about you tell me what's going on in that pretty head of yours?"

"Nothing. I'm fine." There was no way she would tell him her reaction to his nearness had her on edge. She didn't need to stroke his ego. "Let's go."

"Uh-uh. We're not going anywhere until you talk to me."

"James..." She let her voice trail off as she glared at him.

"Sara."

She growled.

A grin spread over his face. "Still cute." He sang the first few bars of "Baby Shark."

"Oh, God, don't you dare!" She smacked his shoulder, some of her anger evaporating as he made her smile with his antics.

He laughed. "That's better. So, you want to tell me now what's going on?"

"No. But I will tell you I'll be fine." She sighed. "I'm just tired." And that wasn't a lie. With so many of her employees out and with the holiday, she was exhausted. It was a big reason why she was having so much trouble compartmentalizing her feelings towards him.

"You sure?"

"Yes. Now drive, please."

He stared at her another moment before putting the car into reverse and backing out of his spot and pointing them toward the church.

Sara leaned her head against the cold window, hoping it would help wake her up. She should have brewed them a thermos of coffee to take. No matter; the church had coffee. It wasn't as good as hers, but it would do.

The drive passed in a blur. She sat up when James pulled in next to her car.

"You sure you're okay to do this? I thought you fell asleep on me."

"No, I'm fine." She unbuckled her seat belt and got out, not waiting for him. Coffee. She needed coffee.

Letting them into the building, she made a beeline for the kitchen and its industrial coffeemaker. With any luck, one of the other volunteers had already started a pot.

The din of voices and laughter registered as she entered the kitchen. Savory scents assailed her nose, relaxing her a bit. Cooking and baking always helped her mood.

"Hey, girl."

Sara smiled at the newly minted sheriff, Katy Lattimer, who stood in front of a large bowl, tearing up loaves of bread for stuffing.

"Hey, yourself. Please tell me there's coffee brewed."

Katy grinned and pointed to her left. "You aren't the only one with more caffeine running through their veins than blood. I haven't slept more than six hours a night since I became sheriff. Most nights I'm lucky to get four."

"You're the sheriff?"

Sara looked over at James. His eyebrows were in his hairline. She understood his surprise. Katy Lattimer was young. And stunning. Barely thirty, the pretty blonde held the highest law enforcement position in the county. She looked more like a model than a cop. But she was shrewd and performed her job with a level of skill many of the other seasoned officers didn't show. It was that skill—and her pristine reputation, something the previous sheriff lacked—that got her appointed to the position when he had a stroke and passed away a month ago.

There were several members of the department unhappy with the county commissioners' decision, but they'd have their say in a couple of years when the previous sheriff's term was up and she had to run in the election. Sara hoped she kicked butt. It was refreshing to have a young woman steering the department and breaking up the good old boys' club.

A predatory look crossed Katy's face as she eyed James from head to toe. Jealousy raised the hairs on Sara's neck and she clenched her fists.

"I sure am." A honeyed smile lit her face. "And who might you be?"

"James O'Malley."

"Wait, are you one of Daisy's brothers?"

"You know my sister?"

"Only in passing. Hard not to when she married our most famous citizen. So, where do you fit in the hierarchy?"

His face relaxed, and he smiled. "I'm the youngest of the boys. Only Daisy's younger."

She opened another loaf of bread and reached inside, pulling out several slices and tearing them apart. "How come you're here with us and not up at the ranch?" Her eyes skittered to Sara. "Though I can probably guess."

Sara blushed and headed for the coffeepot. "He's on a one-man mission to take some of the pressure off of me. All he's really done is give me a headache."

"Oh, come on, Shark. I've been useful and you know it."

Picking up a paper cup, she glanced back at him before turning to pour herself some coffee. "Maybe."

He heaved a sigh, and she didn't have to turn around to see him roll his eyes. It was evident from the sound.

"Whatever."

Katy laughed. "One last question."

"Shoot," James said.

"Why do you call her shark?"

Sara turned around in time to see him arch one of those perfect eyebrows at the sheriff. "You know her. She's tenacious. Not to mention a card shark. She handed me my ass at Uno."

"Oh, that's brilliant." Katy laughed.

A smile twitched Sara's lips. She lifted her coffee cup and took a sip to hide it. There was no way she'd give James the satisfaction of knowing she found him funny right now.

Warmth from the hot brew slid through her. She pushed away from the counter. "And I'll do it again any time, bucko. You lost our rematch, too, remember?"

"Oh, you're on. But since I'm in the hole, I get to pick the game."

"Fine." She strode past him, finding an apron. Glancing up as she tied the strings behind her back, she saw him watching her. "Why are you just standing there? You're here to help, so help."

He held up his hands, a rakish smile slanting his mouth. "Fine."

With a sharp nod, she turned away, fighting a smile.

Fourteen

Bleary-eyed still, James's jaw cracked as he yawned. He felt like his head barely hit the pillow before his alarm blared for him to get up again. But if Sara was arriving at the church this early, then so was he.

Not for the first time, he wondered what the hell he was doing. Yes, he found Sara attractive, but that didn't explain his desire to be her sidekick. Or why he was pushing his writing aside to help her. Sure, he'd gotten some words in, but he could have written another chapter or two in the time he'd been at the diner this past week. He'd tried to stay away, but then her chocolatey eyes and pretty smile would flash in his head and he'd find himself dropping everything to go see her. It just didn't make any sense. Never in his adult life had a woman tied him up and made him want to do things he wouldn't normally do the way Sara Katsaros did.

Travel mug in hand, James climbed into his car. He took a gulp of his coffee, then set the mug in the cup holder and raised the garage door before starting the engine. Asa had moved one of the cars he didn't drive much in the winter into an equipment barn to make room for James's rental. The car was still cold, but not as frigid as it would be if he had to park outside.

He backed out and headed for town, yawning once more. If he'd been sensible, he would have stayed at Sara's last night. They finished at the church around eleven, which meant he didn't get back to the ranch until just after eleven-thirty. By the time he showered and got ready for bed, it was closer to midnight. He'd been up at three-fifteen so he could get to the church again by four.

But he didn't have any extra clothes with him, nor was he going to chance staying in the same house with her. Her sass yesterday left him so revved up, all he could think about was cashing in on their rematch and picking strip poker as his game of choice.

Jeans tightening, he shifted in his seat. Even now, exhausted, the thought of what she'd look like sitting on the floor by the fireplace in just her underwear heated his blood.

His snort filled the car. If he could even win a hand. Knowing his luck, he'd be the one to end up naked while she was still fully clothed.

A wicked smile lifted one side of his mouth. That might work to his advantage. More so than getting her naked. He'd seen the way she stared at him sometimes. How her eyes lingered on his chest when he stretched. Yes, losing at strip poker could be very advantageous.

Another yawn overtook him. That would not happen today, though. They'd likely just fall asleep on each other if they tried.

The drive down the mountain was smooth and uneventful. Slowing down as he crossed the line into town, he went a few more blocks, then turned into the church parking lot. Sara's car was already there, along with one other. He parked next to her and got out.

Finding the door unlocked, he went inside. The murmur

of voices drew him into the kitchen. There, he found Sara and Katy elbow deep in turkeys as they prepped them for cooking.

"That does not look fun." James stared at Sara, who had her arm up the turkey's butt.

She looked up and grinned. "Grab a can of salt and a turkey and try it. It won't take long before you can't feel your fingers anymore and then you won't care."

He wrinkled his nose, but took off his coat and hung it on the rack in the corner. "I think I wore the wrong shirt." He pushed up the sleeves of his henley, but realized they were still going to get coated in turkey juice.

"You can strip," Katy said, a saucy smile on her face. "We won't care."

A blush stole over his cheeks at the sheriff's bold words, matching the one he saw bloom on Sara's face. He chuckled. "No need. I wore a t-shirt underneath." He grabbed his collar behind his neck and pulled to take off the henley. His black undershirt rode up, and he grabbed the hem to pull it down. Sara made a noise, and he looked over to see her quickly look away from his exposed abdomen.

He fought a grin. Yes, losing at strip poker would definitely be advantageous.

∽

Sweaty and tired after a long day, Sara pushed through the back door of the church on her way to the dumpster. Cynthia's numbers had been right; they had a large turnout. But things were winding down now. They'd run out of meat, and there were only a few families left eating. She and the other volunteers had started to clean up so they could go home.

Except she wasn't going home. James had talked her into coming back to the Stone Creek with him for Thanksgiving.

Lifting the lid on the dumpster, she hefted the bag and let it roll over the edge. It landed with a soft thump and the lid banged shut. She wondered if she could renege on him. All she really wanted was to take a hot shower and then sleep.

But he wasn't the only one who would be disappointed if she didn't show up. Daisy would too. And after the tumultuous year the woman had, Sara could put up with some fatigue to not rain on her friend's first holiday celebration as a married woman.

With a sigh, she turned to go back inside, but something behind the dumpster caught her attention. She paused and looked a little closer. It looked like someone tried to throw some old clothes away, but missed. Or maybe someone went dumpster-diving and didn't clean up after themselves. Regardless, she couldn't just leave it there to blow away.

She rounded the dumpster and skidded to a halt, her body freezing at the sight in front of her. A young man laid in a crumpled heap in a puddle of God only knew what that had leaked from the dumpster. His ashen skin and wide, unseeing eyes told her he was long dead.

A scream bubbled up in her throat. It pushed free as her muscles unseized, and she stumbled backward. Her knees buckled, and she put her hands out, catching herself even as she tried to get up and run back to the church. Gravel scrabbled under her shoes as she righted herself. Heart racing—and not from the run—she yanked open the door and ran inside.

The people eating looked up as she entered. She schooled her face and slowed down so she wouldn't alarm any of them, but still speed-walked into the kitchen.

"Katy!"

The woman looked up from washing the stockpot they'd used for mashed potatoes and frowned as she took in Sara's wild expression. "What's wrong?"

"Sara?" James took a step toward her from where he

scraped the dried remains of stuffing from the roasting pans they cooked it in.

"There's—a boy! Behind the dumpster. He's dead."

"What?" The pot thunked against the sink bottom as Katy let it drop so she could rinse her hands. "Tell me what you saw."

"Just that. A boy—young man, maybe." She swallowed hard. James came up beside her and wrapped a hand around her bicep. She leaned into him, finding some strength in his presence. "I put the trash in the dumpster, and as I turned to come back in, I saw a shoe and some fabric. I thought it was trash, so I walked around to pick it up, and that's when I saw him."

"Did you recognize him?" Katy dried her hands.

"Maybe? Not by name, but he looked a bit familiar."

"Okay. Show me."

Sara whirled. James's hand grasped hers, but he didn't stop her, just followed her out, holding on. Her free hand smacked the bar to open the door, and it flew open. They darted through, with Sara leading the way to the dumpster.

"He's back there." She stopped several feet away and pointed, having no desire to see him again.

Katy kept moving. Rounding the dumpster, she stopped, then crouched. "Well, fuck."

"Do you know who it is?" Sara curled her hand into James's shirt.

"Yeah." Katy stood. "It's Hunter Goodman. His dad is one of my deputies. Damn. How did this happen?" She heaved a sigh and pulled her phone from her pocket. "Fuck. I do not want to make this call." Her thumb hovered over device. She cursed again and touched the screen, then put it to her ear and walked away.

"Are you all right?" James grasped her arms and bent to put his face close to hers.

Sara started to nod, but her face crumpled. "No."

"Oh, baby." He pulled her into his chest and wrapped his arms around her.

Her shoulders shook as she cried into his shirt. That poor kid. Now that Katy said his name, she recognized him. He was a senior and friends with the kids who worked for her. She'd seen him come in the diner sometimes when they were working.

Sniffing, she pulled back and wiped her face. "This is terrible. I wonder what happened. How he got back there."

"Did you see any signs of foul play? Blood or bruises?"

She shook her head. "No. If it weren't for his eyes being open, he'd just look like he was sleeping."

"Drugs, maybe?"

Sara shrugged. "I don't know. He didn't seem the type."

"So you do know him?"

She nodded. "Now that I know his name, yes. He's friends with a couple of the kids who work for me. I've seen him at the diner. He seemed like a normal kid."

James glanced at the dumpster, then at Katy as she approached them again.

"Did you talk to his parents?" Sara asked.

A grim set to her face, Katy nodded. "To Jeremiah, yes. I told him to get over here because we have a situation. I'm not breaking that kind of news over the phone. He should be here soon. They don't live too far away. I called in additional units first, though, to help secure the scene."

The first unit's siren split the air as she finished her sentence, pulling into the lot a few moments later. Two more units soon followed. When Jeremiah Goodman arrived, they'd cordoned off the back of the lot.

He rolled to a stop and parked just on the other side of the crime scene tape. The fortyish man who emerged smiled as he spotted his boss. "Hey, Katy, what have we got?" He ducked under the tape, his expression sobering some and a frown forming between his eyes as he took in the deputies standing around, their faces somber as they watched him.

Katy took a breath and faced her deputy. Sara did not envy the woman her job.

"Jeremiah—" she started, cursed, then started again. "There's no easy way to say this, so I'm just going to say it. Hunter—he's dead."

His frown deepened, and anger made his eyes hard. "That's not funny."

"I'm not trying to be. I'm so sorry. Sara found him behind the dumpster when she took out the trash."

He turned his head to look at Sara and James, noticing the tear stains on her cheeks and the redness around her eyes. As the truth sank in, the blood drained from his face, and his eyes swung to the dumpster where a deputy stood guard.

"No."

Tears pricked Sara's eyes again at his broken whisper.

"No, no, no. Not my boy." He took a step forward.

Katy put a hand on his chest. "You don't want to go over there, Jer. This isn't a memory you want."

A lone tear spilled over. "I have to, Katy." He pushed her hand away and hurried past, slowing as he neared the dumpster and saw Hunter's feet peeking out from behind it.

Sara flinched at the wail he let loose as he rounded the edge of the bin. The deputy standing guard caught Jeremiah as he collapsed and wrapped an arm around his waist, holding him. She looked away, unable to watch his pain.

"How about we go inside?" James looped an arm around her waist and turned her toward the church. "It's cold out here, anyway, and neither of us has a coat on."

She nodded and let him lead her in. Numb to the commotion around her, she vaguely heard him tell Katy where they were going.

He led her into the building to a quiet corner, where he pushed her into a chair. "I'm going to get you something hot to drink and take Katy her coat. I'll be right back."

Sara managed to nod, staring blankly up at him. He frowned at her, but walked away. A door opened and closed, letting in the noise from outside, but she paid it little heed. It was like a radio on in the background while she worked—there, but not acknowledged.

Hearing Jeremiah's pain put her mind into protective mode. She'd shut down, refusing to think about what she saw or the family that had just been ripped apart.

~

James hurried back inside the church after taking Katy her coat. A glimpse across the room showed Sara still sitting in the chair he put her in, a stoic mask in place over her face. Worry churned in his gut. He'd never seen her like this. Granted, they'd only known each other a short time, but he never would have thought bright, vibrant, tenacious Sara Katsaros would shut down like this.

His long legs ate up the ground to the kitchen. Cynthia stood in front of one of the coffeemakers, adding water to it. She glanced over as he entered.

"I figured we could all use a little fortification. Since this is a church, I doubted alcohol would be wise, so coffee it is."

He gave the older woman a soft half-smile. "Can I trouble you for a cup for Sara?"

She picked up a paper cup and stepped over to a full urn, pushing the lever. A hot stream of the dark brown brew poured into the cup. "You want one for yourself?" She held out the one she just poured.

"Sure."

She grabbed another cup. "Is it true?"

"Is what true?"

"That it's Hunter Goodman?"

James pressed his lips together and nodded.

"Damn. He was a good boy. I wonder what happened. Does the sheriff have any ideas?"

"No. Sara said there was no blood on his body."

"So, is Katy thinking suicide?"

He shrugged. "I honestly don't know, and I'm not going to speculate. She'll figure it out. I get the feeling she won't quit until she gets Deputy Goodman some answers."

Cynthia poured a third cup and took a sip of the scalding coffee. "You know, she wasn't supposed to be sheriff. It was supposed to be my son."

James raised a brow, wondering where she was going with this.

"I hope she has the skill the county commissioners think she has. They put a lot of trust in her record. I hope it holds up."

"Record?"

"She's a war hero."

"Really?" He could not see that slender, bubbly woman in the midst of war. Sure she was competent and fierce, but a decorated soldier?

"Don't let the blonde hair and bright smile fool you." Cynthia seemed to read his mind. "She's quite the warrior." She shook her head. "She didn't even want the job. Was content with where she was, but the commissioners didn't have a lot of trust in the former sheriff's immediate circle. She was new blood."

"Why not? What was going on?"

"He had a history of letting things slide that probably shouldn't have. And I guess he was screwing the county out of money by fabricating charges to get extra funding, but then using it for his own gain. My boy, Ray, wasn't involved in any of that. He tried to tell the commissioners that, but they refused to listen. Now he's her number two." She shrugged and took another sip of her coffee. "Anyway, I don't know why I'm telling you all of this."

"I think you're just concerned that the truth about what happened to Hunter comes to light."

Her eyes met his. Sadness made their green depths watery. "He was a good boy."

"I'm sorry, Cynthia." He offered her a soft smile, then left her with her thoughts.

Back in the dining area, he headed for Sara, who still sat staring off into space. That worry he felt a few minutes ago escalated. She hadn't moved. Stopping in front of her, he held out the coffee cup. "Here, Shark."

She startled at the sound of his voice, her eyes meeting his, then going to the coffee. "Oh. Thank you." She took it, but didn't drink; just held it in her hands.

James frowned and dragged a chair over. He'd deliberately used the nickname he'd given her, trying to get a reaction. "Hey." He laid a hand over her knee. "Sara, look at me."

Bleak eyes met his.

"Baby, talk to me."

"About what?"

"About what you saw. Get it out. This shutting down thing you're doing isn't healthy."

She stared into her coffee. "I can't think about it. Or talk about it. If I do, I'll break down. You didn't see him." Her voice trailed off into a broken whisper, and she pressed her fist to her mouth.

He rubbed circles on her knee. "I'm sorry it was you who found him. Why didn't you ask me to take out the trash?"

"You were busy." She shrugged. "It was just trash." Her eyes lifted to stare at a point past his shoulder. Taking a deep breath, she sat a little straighter. "I know I need to process it, but I can't do that here. I'm sure I'll have a good cry tonight at home. And I'm afraid Thanksgiving with your family is out. I wouldn't be good company."

"Daisy will get by without us."

Her eyes widened and snapped to his. "What do you mean?"

"If you think I'm leaving you alone after what happened, you've lost your damn mind."

"James, really, I'll be fine alone."

"You need to talk, Sara. You said so yourself. Who are you going to talk to if I don't go home with you? That sickly houseplant in your bathroom?"

That got a rise out of her. Her brows slammed down over her dark eyes and she pierced him with a look that should have withered him where he sat. He was too elated to see something other than that blank expression for it to have much effect on him, though.

"Maybe it would do it some good. I've heard talking to houseplants helps them grow."

"That's singing, Shark."

Her glare intensified at the nickname. He grinned.

"Why are you smiling?"

He held up his hands. "Because you're no longer staring at walls."

Sara's face smoothed out as she thought about his words. He took a sip of coffee, his eyes twinkling above the rim of the cup. James was sure she was cursing him out in her head. She knew he was right; he'd managed to break her out of the trap her mind built around her emotions by goading her.

Annoyance flashed on her face. She crossed an arm over her middle and propped her other elbow on it, taking a drink.

"Look, I'm sorry I annoyed you, but I had to do something to wake you up. You need to deal with the emotions, trust me."

She cocked an eyebrow. "What makes you an expert?"

"Life." He leaned back in his chair and mimicked her pose. "My parents died when I was eighteen. I buried my emotions so deep, I didn't even know where I put them. But they were still there. In every action I took, every stupid decision I made. From not having Daisy's back against our brothers to my choice in women, hell, even my career. Those feeling influenced all of it. And it wasn't until I finally realized I wasn't happy being a lawyer that they reemerged in a way I could see them and deal with them like I hadn't before. I'm still digging my way out of the hole I put them in."

Her head tilted as she stared at him, curiosity showing in the crinkles around her eyes and the purse to her lips. "I didn't lose anyone, though, James. Just saw something horrific."

"I know. And I'm not equating the two." He raised a hand when she started to protest. "Not really. They're the same, but completely different. My point is that strong negative emotions will eat you alive if you let them. It's best to deal with them sooner rather than later. Rip it off like a bandage. The pain fades faster, trust me."

He sat up, putting a hand on her knee again. "I'm coming home with you. If for no other reason than to be there if you want to talk. And if not," he shrugged, a smile breaking free, "we'll play cards."

Fifteen

The sudden quiet as James cut the engine seemed overly loud after the last couple of hours. There had been so many people at the church once word got out about Hunter. Concerned neighbors, friends—they'd all descended on the area. Then there were all the emergency and investigative personnel milling around. Once Katy got their formal statements and told them they could leave, James hadn't hesitated to bundle Sara in her coat and usher her out the door.

They'd taken his car; she was in no shape to drive. The interior light came on as she opened her door. James reached over the seat for the foil-covered pan in the back that Cynthia thrust at them as they left. It contained a sampling of the few leftover sides. There were even two slices of pie. He was thankful she'd thought of them while she and the other volunteers cleaned up. Neither of them had eaten yet. He called Daisy while they waited to give their statements, telling her what happened and that they wouldn't make it to dinner. She offered to bring them each a plate, but he told her they'd figure out something. Cynthia had been that something.

He got out and followed Sara into the house, leaving his coat and shoes near the door.

"I'm going to take a shower." Weariness colored her voice, though he didn't need to hear it to see it all over her face.

"Okay. I'll reheat this and start a fire."

She paused on her way out of the kitchen. "The heat works now." She pointed to the lights above them. "The power's on."

"I know, but I thought the warmth—both literal and figurative—that a fire provides would be comforting."

"Oh. Okay, sure. I'll be back." She left the room.

Sighing, he ran a hand over his face and jaw. Beard stubble rasped beneath his palm, and he took a moment to breathe and sort through his emotions. Sorrow and worry were at the top of the list. But so was determination. He wanted to help Sara get through this, and the best way he knew to do that was to be there when she needed him. And that started with food. Having a full stomach always made everything better.

He moved to the cabinets and took down two plates. Foil crinkled as he lifted it off the dish. His mouth watered as he looked at the array of sides Cynthia packed for them. He knew there wouldn't be any meat, but he was surprised by what they did still have. Stuffing, green beans, sweet potato casserole, and mac and cheese were arranged in neat piles in the pan. She'd put a strip of plastic wrap down in one end and laid two slices of pumpkin pie on it, wrapping it over the top to keep them separate from the other food.

James dug a serving spoon out of the utensil jar next to the stove and split the food between the plates. Not wanting it to get cold if he warmed it up too early, he lit a fire first, then went back to microwave their dinner. When Sara emerged from the bathroom dressed in soft pink sweats and a long-sleeved white tee, they were ready, along with two mugs of hot cocoa.

"Go sit by the fire," he told her as she came into the kitchen. "I'll bring your plate out."

True to form, she ignored him and walked forward to take a plate and mug. "I'm already here."

He rolled his eyes. "Fine." He picked up his own plate and followed her to the living room, settling on the couch, while she tucked herself into an oversize chair.

Wood crackled and popped as it burned, the only sound for several minutes as they ate. James didn't think he was all that hungry until he started eating. Judging from the way Sara dug in, she felt the same. Her initial bite was one of just feeding herself for nourishment. Once the food hit her mouth, though, her hunger kicked in and she polished off her food—pie included—rather quickly.

She set her plate aside, then raised her knees, wrapping her arms around them and resting her chin on top. James got up and took her plate, depositing both in the kitchen before returning to the living room. Her eyes were still on the fire.

"You okay?"

She nodded, but didn't look over. "What do you think happened?"

Instead of going back to the couch, he sat down in front of her on the floor. "I'm not sure. You said there was no blood or visible bruises. Maybe he overdosed."

"Behind a dumpster at a church?"

"I'm just throwing out theories. Maybe he OD'd somewhere else and someone found him and took him there."

"Why wouldn't they just call the police? Or an ambulance?"

"He's a cop's kid. Most people around here probably knew that. If they were doing drugs with him or even supplied them, they would want to be as far removed from the investigation as possible."

"I suppose. It's just weird."

"I agree."

She turned her head, laying her cheek against her knees, and looked at him. "How would you write it?"

James frowned, thinking. "Honestly?"

She nodded.

"I'd write it as a murder."

Sara's dark eyes went wide. "You think Hunter was murdered?"

"I didn't say that. I said that's how I'd write it. It's just weird enough to make a good suspense novel."

"Okay, so how did he die?"

"Drugs injected into his system, or blunt force trauma we couldn't see without moving him."

She turned her head again to stare at the fire. "Well, however he died, I hope it was quick and he didn't feel it."

James agreed. However Hunter Goodman died, he hoped the kid didn't suffer.

With a sigh, he leaned into Sara's chair. To his surprise, she dropped a hand and wove it into his hair. He bit back a moan as she lightly massaged his scalp.

"Thank you."

At her soft words, he glanced up. Her hand slid to the back of his head. "For what?"

"Keeping me company, even though I didn't want it. It's nice not being alone. Having you here is helping me to focus my thoughts."

"Good." He looked back at the fire and pointed at his head. "Keep scratching."

She giggled, which was his goal, and wiggled her fingers.

◦※◦

Darkness greeted James as he opened his eyes. A glance at the clock showed him it was still too early to get up. He lifted his head, listening. What woke him?

A low moan came through the wall, followed by a short cry. He pushed back the covers and padded out of the room. Pausing in front of Sara's door, he grasped the knob. Should he wake her? Maybe she'd settle and go back to sleep. He didn't want to pull her from sleep for a brief nightmare.

A louder cry and a sob came through the door, making his decision for him. It sounded like it was getting worse. He twisted the knob and stepped into her room.

In the glow that spilled in from the hallway nightlight, he could see her tossing and turning on the bed. The blankets wrapped around her legs, and she clutched her pillow. He crossed to her side and laid a hand on her arm. "Sara. Honey, wake up."

Another moan slid past her lips, and he saw a tear leak from her eye. He sat down and shook her harder. "Sara."

She took a deep breath, then stilled as her eyes opened, soon focusing on his face. "James?"

"Hey. You were having a nightmare. I could hear you through the wall. Are you all right?"

"Um, yeah." She tugged at the blankets, pulling them up to cover her torso.

"Do you want to talk about it?"

"Huh?" She looked up from where her eyes were fixed on his chest.

It suddenly occurred to him that he'd run in here without getting dressed. All he had on were his boxer-briefs. Feeling slightly uncomfortable himself, he cleared his throat. "Talk. Did you want to talk about it?"

She shook her head. "No. I was just reliving when I found Hunter."

He nodded. "Okay. Well, I guess I'll let you get back to sleep."

"Okay." She clutched the blanket higher and held his gaze.

Fire lit in James's belly. Coming in here was a mistake. Fresh from sleep, her expression was softer, less wary, as her brain had yet to catch up to her worries. He lifted a hand and wove it into the disheveled curls on the side of her head. She covered it with her own.

He leaned closer. His conscience kicked in just before his lips touched hers. She was an emotional wreck right now. Kissing her—especially when he wasn't wearing anything but underwear—was a terrible idea. He didn't take advantage of women, and if something happened between them right now, that's exactly what he'd be doing.

"I'm sorry." James jerked back and stood. "Goodnight." He didn't wait for her to respond. Just hightailed it back to his room. Closing his door, he leaned against it and blew out a breath. He stared at the bed, gritting his teeth. He didn't want to climb into it alone, but that's the way it had to be. Yanking back the covers, he got in and laid down. Eyes wide open, he stared at the ceiling. He couldn't see anything except Sara's dark eyes in his mind.

Slamming his eyes shut, he rolled to his side, but they didn't go away. With a growl, he sat up and turned on the bedside lamp and reached for his phone. So much for sleeping anymore. Maybe he could get some work done instead. If nothing else, his frustration about not being able to write would take the edge off his desire to go climb into bed with Sara.

He hoped.

Sixteen

Sara stifled a yawn as she poured coffee into a customer's mug. After James woke her from her nightmare, sleep became elusive. She'd laid there, running their encounter through her mind over and over. She still didn't know why he left instead of kissing her, as he so obviously wanted to do. It wasn't like she'd have pushed him away. At first, she'd wondered why he was in her room nearly naked. Then the sight of all that glorious, hair-roughened, muscular chest sent her into an aroused stupor, banishing the horrific images from her dream, and she no longer cared.

But just when she thought he was going to expel all the bad stuff for good, he jerked away and left her high and dry. This morning hadn't been any better. His closed expression over breakfast told her he didn't want to talk about it. The ride to town was a quiet one. He'd pulled into the church parking lot so she could get her car, then told her he had some things to take care of and left. To say she was confused was an understatement.

The cowbell on the door clanged, and Sara looked over to

see Daisy walk in, a frown on her face. Sara excused herself from her customer and walked over to where the other woman sidled up to the counter.

"Hey, you okay?"

"Can we talk?"

"Um," Sara glanced around. She had a full staff today, so things were running smoothly. "Sure. Come on." She tipped her head toward the kitchen, then led Daisy through to the back to her office.

Daisy shut the door behind her and dropped into the guest chair as Sara sat down at the desk.

"What's up?"

"What did you do to my brother?"

Sara frowned. "What do you mean?"

"I mean, he showed back up this morning, looking like a surly bear. I tried to ask him about what happened yesterday, but all he said was, 'I don't want to talk about it,' then traipsed up to his room. When I tried to peek in on him at lunchtime to see if he was hungry, he told me he'd get something later and didn't even look up from his laptop."

Apparently, writing was the stuff he had to do, Sara thought. "I didn't do anything to him."

Daisy studied her for a moment. "Did something happen between you? Did you have a fight?"

"No."

The other woman narrowed her eyes.

Sara let out a soft chuckle and held up her hands. "I swear. Nothing out of the ordinary happened." *Except him coming into my room in those skintight boxer-briefs.* "We parted on good terms this morning. Maybe he's just feeling the pressure to get his book done. He's supposed to go back to Chicago on Sunday. Could be he feels like he needs to accomplish more on this retreat of his than what he has."

Suspicion crept into Sara's head as she talked. Had their

encounter last night got to him more than what he let on? Was that why he ran off so fast? But why would a look in the dark affect him more than the few intense kisses they'd shared?

She didn't have the answers, and she was too tired to care. What did it matter, anyway? He was leaving in two days.

"Yeah, maybe." Daisy tapped her chin, her brow creased in thought. "He's just acting strange. I hoped you could shed some light on his behavior."

"Nope, sorry. Whatever's going on in that pretty head of his is a mystery to me too."

Daisy sighed. "That's what I was afraid of."

"Why are you so concerned? He's an adult and can handle his own problems."

"I know, but that doesn't mean I don't care. Of all my brothers, I relate to James the most because we're closest in age. And he got a bit of a taste of the others' meddling."

That was news to Sara. "He did?"

"Yeah. They're the reason he went to law school. He always liked psychology better. And he really just wanted to write. Though, I guess school was good for something. It gave him the insight and skills to write thrillers and provided a stable income while he got established." She frowned. "It also gave him a good poker face."

Sara giggled as she remembered playing cards with him. "It's not as good as you'd think."

Daisy laughed. "Probably not. I'm just a little out of touch with him. We're working on that."

"Good."

"Good?" Daisy straightened. "Boy, he really has changed your opinion of him. Last week, you were ready to put him back on a plane to Chicago."

"I know, but I've gotten to know him. He's trying to earn your trust."

Daisy smiled. "Yeah. They all are. I'm glad I came here. It's been life-changing in more ways than I could have ever hoped."

Sara leaned forward and wrapped her friend in a hug. "I'm glad too. I've needed a friend like you, but I didn't realize it until you got here. Thank you for telling your brothers to shove it."

"You're welcome." Daisy hugged her back, then let go. "So, did you just come here to ask me about James?"

"No. I also came for a milkshake. I can't make them like you do."

Sara grinned and stood. "It's probably the ice cream. You can't get what I buy from the grocery store."

"Sneaky." Daisy followed her out.

Laughing, Sara led her into the freezer to get the chocolate ice cream, then went to the blender.

"I hope you realize, now that you've shown me how to make this, I might just come back here all on my own and do it myself in the future."

Sara shrugged. "Fine by me." She scooped ice cream into the blender, then added milk and chocolate syrup before putting on the lid and pressing start. The machine whirred to life, quickly blending the ingredients into a thick shake. Daisy fetched a to-go cup, and Sara poured the mixture into it.

Unwrapping a straw, Daisy stuck it through the lid and took a deep draw. "That's so good." She turned and headed for the door. "I better pay for this and go. You need to get back to work, and I want to hit up a couple of shops while I'm here. See if I can find some presents for Nori and my sisters-in-law." She glanced back. "You're lucky. You only have your parents to buy for. I have about a bazillion in-laws and nieces and nephews, plus my brothers."

"Hey, we should take a trip to Billings next week and go shopping. Tuesdays are usually slow. What do you say?"

"Sure. That sounds fun. I'll see if Marci wants to come,"

she said, mentioning the Stone Creek foreman's wife and their friend.

"Okay. We'll figure out times closer to then."

"All right, sounds good."

Sara rung her up, then waved as she left. Her spirits were buoyed by Daisy's visit. It would be nice to get out of her normal routine for a day. With all her staff back, she could afford to take some time for herself.

The bell sounded again, and she looked up. The sheriff walked in, wearing a scowl that did not match her pretty face.

"Katy, hi."

"Hi, Sara." The woman strode up to the counter. "I just came to give you an update and to ask you a couple of other questions."

"Okay. Do you want to go in the back where it's more private?" She tipped her head toward the kitchen, then glanced at the dining room, which had gone quiet at her entrance.

Katy looked over at the other patrons and nodded. "Yeah, that might be best."

Sara pushed through the kitchen door again, beginning to feel a bit like it was a revolving door, and entered her office. She motioned for Katy to sit, then perched in her own chair. "So, what have you found out?"

The sheriff sat, adjusting her coat and gun belt. "Preliminary autopsy results indicate he died from several hard blows to the chest. His sternum's broken into pieces and a couple of them pierced his heart. He bled out internally."

Sara gasped. That poor child! "How did that happen?"

Katy shrugged. "Don't know. We went back to the dumpster to look for a weapon, but didn't find anything that matched the wound pattern. Did you notice anyone or anything out of the ordinary? Either then or earlier?"

Did she? Sara searched her memory of the incident and of

the day, but nothing came to mind. "No. The only thing out of place was Hunter."

"No people walking by or strange cars?"

"Honestly, I don't know. I know there wasn't anyone outside when I took out the trash. We'd run out of meat, so we closed up and only had a few people left inside still eating. And there were cars in the parking lot, but I can't tell you if any of them didn't belong."

"Damn, I was afraid you'd say that." Her eyebrows dipped. She propped her elbow on the chair's arm and ran a finger over her top lip, thinking. "Did you see Hunter earlier in the day? Or any of his friends, maybe?"

Sara wracked her memory again, but still came up with little. "There were a few high school students there with their families. None of them were alone. I don't remember seeing Hunter. How did his parents not know he wasn't home?"

"He was supposed to be at his girlfriend's." Katy pinched the bridge of her nose. "The girl said he never showed up, so she thought he changed his mind. They had a fight the night before, so she didn't think much of it. Just sent him a few nasty-grams, telling him what she thought of his no-show behavior." She let out a sigh. "I don't suppose you guys kept a list of everyone who came, did you?"

"No."

"I was afraid you'd say that too." She sighed again and stood. "I'm going to track down the other volunteers and see if they remember anything. Can you make me a list of everyone who came in that you can remember? I need to talk to as many of them as possible and see if they saw anything. That boy didn't just appear behind that dumpster."

"No, he did not."

Katy reached for the doorknob. "Thanks for your help, Sara."

"Of course. Katy."

The sheriff glanced back, standing in the doorway.

"Will you keep me informed? I'd like to know what happens."

"As much as I can, yes." She offered Sara a soft smile. "Get me that list."

Seventeen

Flurries drifted through the air to land on James, melting as they made contact. He huddled deeper into his coat, shielding himself from the wind as he crossed the street from his parking spot to the sheriff's department. Katy Lattimer called the ranch and asked him to come in, so here he was.

Inside the building, he gave his name to the deputy at the desk, who had him sign a logbook, then gave him a visitor's badge. James followed the man through the door to his right and to a conference room down the hall. He sat in a chair around the long table and looked out the window at the squirrels chasing each other through the bushes as he wondered what this was about.

The door swung open, and the sheriff entered, her blonde hair pulled up into a high ponytail. She had a file folder and a notepad in her hands. "Mr. O'Malley, thank you for coming in."

"Of course. You said you had some questions you wanted to ask? Did something come up or was my statement not clear?"

She smiled and shook her head as she sat down across from

him. "No, your statement was fine. We have some new information on the case, so I'm re-interviewing everyone."

"Oh? What kind of information?"

"Preliminary autopsy results. Hunter died from internal blood loss after a blow to his chest fractured his sternum and the pieces pierced his heart."

James wrinkled his nose. That sounded horrible. "That's awful. So, what can I help you with?"

"We didn't find a weapon on-site, so he was likely dumped there. Did you notice anyone out of the ordinary? Or a car that shouldn't have been there?"

His mouth flattened. "Doubtful. I'm not from around here, so I don't know the locals the way the other volunteers do. Everyone looked unfamiliar to me. Nothing struck me as strange, though."

She studied him a moment, her honey-colored eyes locked on his. "You were an attorney, right?"

A frown drew down his eyebrows. "Yes. What does that have to do with anything?"

"Nothing, really. Just looking for insights. I have to confess, I looked you up. You were a criminal prosecutor before you left that life to write full time. What does this situation say to you? Anyone you think I should look into? I'll be honest. I've never worked a homicide before. None of us in the department have. It just doesn't happen around here. And my only true investigator, Mike Swanson, is out on family medical leave because his wife was just diagnosed with breast cancer. So anything you can offer, I'm listening."

James's eyes roved her face as he considered her request. The police didn't normally ask for his help. Usually it was the other way around, and he was researching a book or, in his previous life, working on a case. But she seemed sincere. "Cynthia said you were in the military. I'm guessing that meant military police?"

Katy nodded. "I did six years active duty—the last two as a dog handler—before an injury sidelined me. I spent the final two years of my enlistment on reserve duty and went to school to get my criminal justice degree. I've been with this department in some capacity for seven years. All I've ever wanted to be is a cop."

"And you never handled any homicides as an MP?"

She shook her head. "Any cases I worked where death was involved were related to terrorist activities. Stateside, I worked gate security. Overseas, I did pretty much the same thing, but they'd also take me into the field because my dog was trained to sniff out explosives." Her expression grew tight.

James realized there was a story there—one she didn't want to talk about—so he didn't press. "Okay, well, normally, I'd look at the significant other first, but I can't see a teenage girl bashing her boyfriend's chest in, so she probably didn't do it. Her dad, maybe? Then I'd look at his friends or kids at school with whom he didn't get along well."

She nodded as he talked. "That's pretty much where I was going to start. His parents said he wasn't into anything illicit, but teenagers are good at hiding things."

"Are you sure his dad just didn't want to see it? I mean, he's a cop, after all. How would it look if his son was a junkie?"

Her lips flattened, and she sat back in her chair, folding her hands over her abdomen. "That's a valid point. I'll make sure to ask Hunter's friends about drug use and talk to Jeremiah again."

James hesitated. More than likely it was his own dislike of the man that brought him to mind, but he couldn't shake the feeling that there was something seriously off about him. "Have you considered Billy Jeffries as a suspect?"

"Billy Jeffries? No. Why?" Her gaze sharpened.

"What do you know about him?" he countered.

"Not a whole lot. He's lived here as long as I can remember, but I know he wasn't born here. He's a war vet. Lives up the mountain where he raises some livestock. He pretty much keeps to himself. What makes you suspect him?"

"I'm not sure. There's just something about him that's setting off my internal radar. He always seems to be around whenever I'm with Sara. And he looks like a bum, but his eyes say he's anything but."

Katy picked up a pen and made a note. "I'll look into him, but without something connecting him to Hunter, there isn't much I can do."

"I know. Just keep an eye on him is all I'm saying. Does he have a record?"

"I don't know." She sat up and logged into her computer, where she entered Jeffries's name into the database. "Nope. Clean as a whistle."

James frowned. That didn't make sense. Something about that guy was hinky. "Okay." He edged forward in his chair, ready to get up. "Did you have any other questions?"

"No, not at the moment. When are you leaving?"

"I'm supposed to go home Sunday, but I've been thinking about staying longer."

She nodded. "Just let me know what you decide."

"I will. Thanks for the info."

"Yep."

James rose and left her office, exiting the station. In his car, he started the engine, then sat there, thinking. Who would want to kill a seventeen-year-old kid? And in such a brutal way?

As he shifted the car into reverse to back out of his space, he saw his sister walk out of a storefront and down the sidewalk. She had several bags in one hand and her cane in the other. He shut the car off and hopped out before she could get far.

"Daisy."

She paused, glancing back. A half-smile kicked up one side of her face as he jogged across the street. "Hey. You come out of your cave finally?"

"Yeah. Sheriff Lattimer called and asked me to come answer some questions. I see you decided to hit up some Black Friday sales." He reached for her packages.

"Thanks." She handed over the bags. "I wanted to see how Sara was doing, then figured since I was here, I might as well do some shopping. Want to walk around with me?"

The mention of Sara's name put a frown on his face, but he quickly wiped it away. He didn't want Daisy asking questions about their relationship. He didn't have any answers to give her. "Sure. Who are we shopping for?"

Daisy grinned. "Sara."

He blinked down at her, and she laughed.

"Relax. I need to shop for Marci too. And Shelly. I got the other wives done."

"What about Aunt Nori?"

"I found a scarf I think she'll like, but I want to get her something else too. I just don't know what. I need to look for some of the kids too."

James held out an arm. "Well, let's go see what we can find."

Smile growing, she looped her now free hand through his elbow.

"Where to first?"

She shrugged. "Wherever strikes our fancy. Pine Ridge has a lot of neat little shops."

"Yeah. It's a big switch from Chicago, where shopping downtown means Saks and Neiman Marcus."

"I much prefer the shopping here."

James did too. But then, he didn't like shopping in general.

They ducked into a home décor store. Daisy only made it a few steps before she squealed and hurried toward a display against the wall. She stopped in front of a rack of long boards that looked like rulers.

"Who's that for?"

"Marci. It's a growth chart. Her baby, Sloan, can stand now, so this would be great." She glanced at him, then turned back to the boards. "Which color do you think would be best? Cream or gray?"

He walked closer. "I don't know. I'm assuming you hang this since the first six inches are missing from the bottom? What color are her walls?"

"Oh, good point. They're gray, so the cream would be best."

James picked up a cream chart.

"Well, that was easy. Let's see if I can find anything else in here." Daisy planted her cane and pivoted, off to the next display in a blink.

He couldn't help the smile that lifted one corner of his mouth at the way she used that cane to her advantage. Idly, he wondered if she used it the way their grandmother used to, and smacked peoples' legs when they annoyed her.

Snickering quietly, he followed her around the store. She picked out a couple more small things, then checked out.

"Are you going to make me carry this all over town, or can I run across the street and put it in my car?" He gestured to the board in his hands.

"You can put it away, sure." Her phone beeped from her purse. She opened the bag to dig it out.

James left her to it and jogged across the road to put the sign away. When he turned back, she wasn't on her phone, but talking to a blonde woman on the sidewalk who looked familiar. From the set to both their faces, it wasn't a pleasant conversation. He waited for a truck to pass, then jogged back to his sister's side.

"Everything okay?" He studied the woman now smiling at him like she wanted to eat him. She was pretty, but something about her had him hanging a no-fly zone sign around her neck.

"It's fine. Marla just stopped to—admire the scenery." Daisy sneered at the other woman.

"It's mighty fine." Her blue eyes raked over him from head to toe.

He suppressed a shudder. There had been a time he wouldn't have minded her blatant appraisal, but he'd long outgrown the need to screw every pretty woman he met.

"How Daisy comes from a family with a brother as handsome as you, I'll never know." She offered him a sexy smirk. "You wanna buy me a drink later?"

"No."

Her smile faltered as surprise flickered in her eyes. She scowled. "Well, now I see the resemblance. You're as rude as your sister." She stomped away, entering a store a few doors down.

"Who was that?"

Daisy rolled her eyes. "Marla Wilkins."

He frowned. That name sounded familiar. "Why do I know that name?"

"She's the woman who gave the interview to the tabloids, claiming she and Asa were in a relationship."

"She looks broken-hearted."

Daisy giggled. "For sure." She threaded her arm through his again and pulled him down the sidewalk.

"She's the one who keyed your car too, right?"

"Yep. She's a menace. Which is why we're walking right past her store."

James's eyebrows shot up. "She's a business owner?"

"Yes. Apparently, her brain didn't extend to relationship choices."

He barked a quick laugh. "I guess not."

They passed Marla's resale store and turned into the next one. Curiosity piqued James's interest as he looked around. Eclectic was a good word for the place. It was a hodge-podge of vintage and new, home décor and clothing. It even had a children's toy section toward the back.

Daisy wandered off to one side to look at a collection of vases. He wandered toward the rear of the store. He hadn't bought any presents yet for his nieces and nephews, so the toys were calling his name. Perusing the shelves, he noted the unconventional nature of many of the items. Instead of Barbies and plastic play sets, the store stocked wooden food sets, boutique mini animal dolls, and STEM toys. It also had a small selection of plush toys.

He grabbed a mini doll set for Brian's youngest. Sabrina would love the cat family and their little cottage. He also picked out some magnet tile sets for Kyle's twins.

James turned to go find Daisy. His gaze moved past the plush toys as he did so, and he stopped as one of them caught his attention. It was a shark.

"Oh, she'll kill me," he muttered to himself. But he had to. The twelve-inch Great White called to him with its toothy grin. Not second-guessing himself, he plucked it off the pile and added it to his stack, then went to find his sister.

"I see you decided to do some shopping of your own." Daisy smiled at him as he approached her.

"Yep. They've got some nice toys."

"You leave anything back there for me?"

He shrugged. "Go look."

"I will. Help me decide." She held up two small dishes. One was cream with pink and yellow roses painted on it. The other was a jade green with similar colored flowers. "Which one do you think Shelly would like more? They're jewelry trays."

"Hell, I don't know. I like the green. Looks less grandma-ish."

"Hmm. Fair point." She put the cream dish back on the shelf. "Green it is." Turning, her gaze landed on the pile in his arms, and she frowned. "Who's the shark for?"

James couldn't stop his grin. "Sara."

Confusion lit Daisy's eyes. "Why?"

"It's an inside joke. We played a lot of cards while we were holed up together, and she kicked my ass every time."

She still looked confused.

"Card shark?" he said.

Her face brightened. "Oh. Okay." She rolled her eyes. "Original."

"Whatever. It's funny. She'll kill me and we'll both enjoy it. Go finish your shopping."

Daisy giggled, waggling her eyebrows. "You'll both enjoy it, huh? What exactly is going on with you two?"

"Nothing." James glanced away.

"Uh-huh. That's what she said too. You should just quit fighting it. Everyone can see you like each other."

"It's not that simple, Dais."

"Sure it is. It's everything else that's complicated."

"Exactly. Can we finish shopping now?"

She huffed. "Fine." She walked deeper into the toy section.

James picked up the shark and stared into its beady glass eyes. Maybe he should put it back. He wasn't lying when he said his relationship with Sara was complicated. And he couldn't help but wonder if he was making a mistake. Was it wise to start something—or continue something—with a woman he probably would only see a handful of days a year? As he laid alone in the dark last night, he'd wondered what to do about his growing feelings for her. When he dropped her off this morning, he wasn't any closer to an answer.

He still wasn't, but that didn't stop him from putting the shark back onto his pile, or the smile that spread over his face as he thought about how she'd react to the gift. "What do you say, Killer? Think she'll like you?" He stared into the shark's glossy black eyes and nodded once. "Yeah, she will." He knew she'd pretend not to, but he'd seen the smile the last time he used the nickname. Regardless of what developed between them romantically, he knew she liked him as a friend. And for a friend, he'd buy a goofy toy that made her laugh any day of the week.

Eighteen

The doorbell chimed through the house, interrupting Sara's leisurely bath. She opened her eyes and glared at the row of candles sitting on the ledge. Who the hell was ringing her doorbell at ten o'clock on a Friday night? It had been a long-ass day, and all she wanted was to relax in the warm water, then go to bed.

The bell chimed again, more insistently this time, as the person on the other side of the door pressed the button multiple times in succession.

"Dammit." Water sloshed as Sara stood up and stepped out of the tub. "This better be important." Though the fact that it was so late told her it probably was. Sighing as she reached for a towel, she dried off, then threw on her thick, mint-green terrycloth robe and exited the bathroom.

Cold air hit her as she yanked the front door open to see James standing on her porch. The smile on his face vanished as he took in her attire. Sara blushed as she saw the heat flare in his eyes.

"What are you doing here? And so late?"

"Huh?" His eyes shot to hers. "Oh, um" he cleared his throat, "can I come in?"

She stared at him a moment before stepping back. "Only because it's cold and I don't feel like having this conversation in the doorway while I freeze my butt off." And she was. The robe was thick, but she didn't have a stitch on underneath it. A cold draft had found her nether regions.

He stepped inside and shut the door. "Thanks."

Sara crossed her arms. She knew he couldn't see her beaded nipples through the heavy fabric, but it didn't change the fact she felt exposed. "Why are you here?"

"I brought you something." He lifted his hand from behind his back. A flowered gift bag hung from his fingers.

She frowned at the bag. "What's this?"

He shrugged. "Just something I found in town today." He narrowed his eyes. "Why are you being so hostile?"

Huffing, she let her arms drop. "I'm not. But it's late and I was in the bath."

James cleared his throat. "Oh. Um, sorry. I didn't mean to interrupt." He dropped his arm. "I can come back tomorrow. Or even stop up at the café. It's not important, really."

She rolled her eyes. "You're here, so what's in the bag?"

"Just something I saw while shopping with Daisy." He held it up. "It reminded me of you."

"One question." She took the sack. "Why couldn't it wait?"

James rocked back on his heels and put his hands in his pockets. "I was in the area?"

Sara giggled and rooted through the tissue paper. "Out for another jog?"

He laughed. "Not hardly. I was stuck on my novel again, so I decided to go for a drive. I saw your present as I was leaving my room and figured I'd stop by."

Her hand encountered something soft. Lifting it from the

bag, she blinked. A stuffed shark? He bought her a stuffed shark? A soft giggle slipped past her lips. She tried to stifle it, but couldn't. Another one slid out until she gave a full laugh. His low chuckle joined hers.

"A shark, really?"

"I named him Killer."

She giggled again. "Where did you find this?"

"That place across from the sheriff's department that sells a mix of everything. Secret Garden."

"I can't believe you bought me a stuffed shark. I hate that nickname."

He took a step forward, invading her space. "No you don't. You just want to."

Her giggles died at his nearness. "And why would I want to do that?"

"To keep me at arm's length. Newsflash," he shuffled closer, "it's not working."

The shark squished beneath her fingers as she gripped it tighter. Her breath caught in her chest, leaving her completely as he cupped her jaw.

"James."

His bright blue eyes glittered with need. Sara felt an answering desire low in her belly.

"If you want me to leave, kick me out now. Before I kiss you."

Would it be so bad if she gave in to the need? To have a fling with him before he went back to his life and she went back to hers without him? She didn't want a relationship. With him leaving, it was the perfect way to scratch an itch that hadn't been scratched in a very long time. And she had a feeling he'd be particularly good at scratching that itch.

The bag crinkled as she slipped the shark back into it. Tossing it down, she inhaled a shaky breath and put a hand on the knot of her robe. His eyes strayed to her waist, widening as he watched her fingers untie the belt.

"Sara." Grit made his voice lower than normal.

She shivered at the sound.

"I didn't come here for this."

"Then why did you come?"

"Because I wanted to see you." His eyes met hers, and he lifted his other hand to frame her face. "And to spend time with you."

"Well, you're going to get your wish. You're going to see all of me. And it'll take hours for you to explore." The knot slid free, and the two ends of the belt dangled at her sides.

James looked down at where the robe gaped. Heat suffused her skin as he trailed a finger down her neck, over her collarbone, and into the gap. Her nipples beaded to hard points and moisture pooled between her legs.

"Are you sure?"

She took hold of his hand and slid it under her robe to cup her breast. "I'm sure."

His mouth crashed onto hers. Sara wove her hands into his hair, every cell in her body focused on him, and held on as he wrapped his arms around her waist and carried her toward her bedroom. As they passed the bathroom, some of the fog cleared when she smelled the scented candles she had burning.

"Wait." She pushed out of his arms to hurry into the room to blow them out and drain the tub. Spinning around, she grinned. "Where were we?"

The blue of his eyes had all but disappeared as his pupils dilated with arousal. They were locked on her torso, which was more exposed now, thanks to her movements. Sara shrugged her shoulders and let the robe drop to the ground.

"Jesus." James marched forward and scooped her into his arms, sealing his mouth to hers once more. Stumbling out of the room, he got them into her bedroom, setting her on her feet beside the bed.

"You're wearing way too many clothes," she muttered against his mouth. Her fingers found the zipper on his coat and pulled it down.

He let go of her to take it off. Sara didn't wait. She attacked the button on his jeans and yanked the zipper down over his burgeoning erection. More moisture pooled between her legs as she got an idea of what waited for her.

With a groan, he pushed her hands away and took a step back to undo his shoelaces and toe off his boots. He pulled his shirt over his head, then shoved his pants and underwear down his legs. Sara's eyes widened as she took him in. *Oh, this was going to be so good.*

She reached out and cupped him, eliciting another groan. When she squeezed, he tipped his head back and his mouth fell open. Wondering what other sounds she could get out of him, she dropped to her knees.

"Sara? What are you doing?"

She just hummed and glanced up as she closed her mouth around the tip of him. He made a strangled sound, and both his hands landed in her hair, gripping it tight. She took him deeper and bobbed once. He growled and pulled her away.

"You can do more of that later. I'm too close to the edge for you to continue." He didn't wait for her to respond. Instead, he lifted her off her feet and tossed her onto the mattress.

She scooted up to the pillows, and he crawled after her, latching onto her mouth again. Spreading her knees, she cradled him between her thighs. He teased her entrance, sending waves of heat through her body. She craved this man like nothing else. He'd barely touched her and she wanted him any way she could have him so long as it was now.

He seemed to sense her urgency and lifted his head. He

stroked himself through her wetness and grinned as she moaned. "Now who's the tease?"

"James, please."

"Not yet, baby. Not yet." He bent his head to suckle her breast and ground against her.

Her core pulsed, and she moaned again. Dear God. What was happening? She never got this hot this fast.

He nipped her breast, and she cried out.

"Too hard?"

Head thrashing against the pillow, she clutched him to her chest. "No." She felt him smile, and he moved to her other breast.

"You smell good. Like lavender."

"It's my bath wash."

"Mmm... I like it." He sucked her breast into his mouth and teased the tip with his tongue.

Another moan slid past her lips. She trailed her hands down the back of his neck and over his shoulders to trace the dips and valleys of his muscular arms. Touching him helped to ground her some, and she brought her hands around to his sides, feeling the bone and sinew under his silky skin. The man was perfection. She still had a hard time believing he sat behind a computer all day, writing. She wasn't complaining, though. Not when that perfect body was doing everything in its power to make her feel amazing.

He moved away from her chest to slide lower, teasing her navel, then the thatch of dark hair at the apex of her thighs. His tongue slid into the valley to touch the sensitive flesh hiding there, and Sara thought she'd rocket through the ceiling. Her hips bucked into his face, and he grasped them to hold her still as he licked and teased her folds. When he slid a finger into her, she flew over the edge with a howl.

"That's what I was waiting on." James sat up with a grin.

Through hooded eyes, she ran her eyes over his powerful

physique, pausing on his hard shaft jutting out from a patch of dark hair at his hips. "You gonna use that or just tease me all night?" She tipped her head toward his erection.

His nostrils flared. "Oh, we're going to use it, all right." He started to lean over her and then paused, frowning. "As soon as we find some protection."

She pointed at the bedside table, blushing. "I bought them on a whim after you stayed here the first time. My brain wanted to think this wouldn't happen, but my body knew better. I'm weak when it comes to"—she motioned to his naked body—"this."

He grinned as he leaned over to remove the box of condoms from the drawer. "I'm not complaining." Tearing a packet off the strip, he sheathed himself, then moved between her legs.

Sara's eyelids fluttered, and she tipped her head back as he probed her entrance.

"Baby, look at me." He thrust a hand into her hair, tilting her head toward him. "I want to see your eyes."

She met his gaze, seeing the passion and need she felt reflected in his eyes. He pushed forward, easing into her. Sara gasped, but didn't break eye contact. Even as her eyes widened at the intrusion, she held his gaze until he was seated fully within her.

He only gave her seconds to adjust before he pulled back, then thrust hard, touching her womb. All thought fled her brain as her eyes rolled back in pleasure. "Do that again."

"Yes, ma'am."

Sara lifted her legs to lock her ankles around his waist as he thrust into her again. And again and again. Moaning, she held on as he took her to a plane of existence she didn't know was possible. Thrust after thrust sent her spiraling up the mountain and into the stars until she finally broke. Waves of pleasure, one after the other, crashed over her. She let loose with a shout and did her best to keep her head above water. James stiffened above her, then his hoarse cry mingled with hers before he stilled.

Together, they sagged into the mattress, chests heaving as they tried to catch their breath.

"Wow." James lifted his head from her breasts to look at her.

"Wow, indeed. Can we do that again?"

He chuckled and rolled to her side. "Yeah. Just give me a couple of minutes."

She lifted a finger, swallowing to bring some of the moisture back to her mouth. "Yeah. But only a few."

Nineteen

Soft hands slid around James's waist and even softer lips pressed into the space between his shoulder blades. A smile lifted his mouth, and he glanced over his shoulder to see Sara standing behind him. "Coffee?"

"Does it come with a side of you?"

He set the carafe back on the warming plate and spun around to hold her close, locking his hands behind her waist and running his thumbs in small circles in the soft terrycloth of her robe at the top of her butt. "I think that can be arranged." James swelled behind the fly of his jeans, and he leaned down. "We don't have to have all our fun in one day, though."

Her hands slid into his hair, and a slight frown wrinkled her forehead. "What do you mean? You're leaving tomorrow."

"Actually, I'm staying a little longer."

She stiffened in his arms. "What?"

"Hunter Goodman's case has me curious. And cautious. Plus, I'm finding the atmosphere around here has been good for me and my writing. Yesterday notwithstanding. Honestly, I was more distracted by thoughts of you, which is what prompted me to come over here." He leaned down to kiss her, but she slid a hand between them, covering his lips.

"You're staying?"

It was his turn to frown. "Yes?"

"No." Pulling her hand away, she backed out of his embrace. "Why?"

"I just told you why." Confused, he crossed his arms and stared at her. "You seem upset. Why? I thought you'd be happy about that after last night."

Eyes widening, she put a hand on the counter. "Please tell me you didn't decide to stay because of me."

"What? No. Not completely. I was already pretty certain I was going to stay yesterday afternoon. But I won't lie and say you didn't factor into my decision." Why was she so upset he was staying? He thought she'd welcome the chance for them to spend more time together.

Sara groaned and covered her face. "No. You're supposed to leave. This was just supposed to be a fling."

Hurt sucker-punched James in the gut. "A fling? I'd call it a one-night stand except you wanted to play monkey in the middle again this morning until you found out I'm not leaving." He pushed away from the counter, coffee forgotten. He didn't need it to wake up now. "It would have been nice to know this was nothing more than a quick slap and tickle before the slap or the tickle." Shaking his head, he stormed past her to find his shirt and shoes.

"James, wait."

He kept walking. If she wanted to talk, she could do it while he dressed.

"James, I'm sorry. I just—I thought you were safe. That we could"— she waved her hand around in a circle—"you know, and then I could let you go."

"Did it occur to you that maybe I wanted more than,"— he mimicked her arm movement—"you know?"

She frowned at him. "Why?"

Bending, he snatched his t-shirt from the floor, then stared at her, incredulous. "Why not? I might flirt, and I know you think I think I'm God's gift to women, but that doesn't mean I have a string of one-night stands, nor that I don't want something more meaningful. I'm thirty-six, Sara. All of my siblings are married now, and they all have kids except Daisy, though I doubt it'll be long before she joins that party. I want more than just a roll in the sheets." With jerky movements, he pulled his shirt on and thrust his arms into the sleeves. "I thought you might want the same. I see we should have had this conversation before we screwed each other's brains out."

Sitting on the edge of the bed, he pulled on his boots, tying them with quick, jerky movements. He couldn't help but notice she stayed silent after his tirade. Grabbing his sweater, he stood. Shoulders set, he stalked toward her in the doorway and lifted an eyebrow, silently asking if she had anything to say.

Her jaw worked, and she stepped aside. "I'm sorry."

"Don't be." He offered her a toothy, cold smile. "It was fun, right?" Smile dying, he didn't wait for a response. Just left her standing there in that damn mint-green robe that started it all.

∽

The clang of her metal spatula against the grill top was louder than usual as Sara scrambled eggs. Normally, cooking was cathartic, but not today. It didn't matter how much or how hard she chopped or sliced, her anger stayed the same.

How dare he place the blame for their encounter on her? He knew she thought he was leaving. What did he think she wanted from him? A long-distance relationship? Hell, no.

Metal on metal clanged again.

"I think they're done, Sara."

"What?" She glanced over at her line cook, Melody.

"The eggs." Melody pointed at the grill. "I think they're done."

Sara looked down at the eggs now pummeled to small bits on the grill. Brown tinged most of the pieces. They were ruined. "Oh, right." She scraped the whole mess to the back of the grill and scooped it up, tossing it in the trash.

"What's wrong with you? You've hardly said two words all morning. Better yet, what are you even doing here? You weren't supposed to come relieve me until this afternoon."

"I got bored at home." Sara cracked two eggs into a bowl and whipped them with a fork, then poured them onto the grill.

Melody chuckled. "I'm sure you did. You're a workaholic. Why didn't you go find that handsome brother of Daisy's? Spend some time with him."

Anger surged again. Metal clanged once more as she chopped up the eggs.

"Whoa." Melody took two steps toward Sara and removed the spatula from her hand. "Let's not ruin another batch. I take it your mood has to do with said handsome brother?"

"No."

Melody arched an eyebrow.

Sara sighed. "Maybe." She took the spatula back and gave the eggs another scramble, then picked up a plate and scooped them onto it. "I don't want to talk about it, though."

Something smacked the kitchen door, making it fly open. Sara looked over to see Daisy walk in, leaning on her cane as she maneuvered over the tile floor.

The smile on Sara's face died a swift death at the scowl on Daisy's.

"Did you sleep with my brother and then show him the door? Because he did the walk of shame this morning, but he wasn't smiling. In fact, he looked ready to hurt someone."

"Jesus, Daisy. Keep your voice down." Sara handed Melody her spatula, then ushered Daisy to her office.

"Answer my question." Daisy's eyes shot fire as Sara closed the door.

"It's complicated."

"Uncomplicate it."

Sara sighed and sank into her desk chair. "Sit down."

Daisy plopped into the guest chair with a huff.

"He showed up at my house last night with some stupid stuffed shark he found shopping yesterday with you. One thing led to another, and we ended up in bed."

"Why? You were dead set against anything more than friendship with him."

"That's the complicated part. He's just so damn hot. And funny, and smart, and just nice. I still didn't—don't—want a relationship, but I knew he was leaving, so it felt safe. I wanted just a piece to bring out on long days to buoy my spirits. To bring out on nights when I felt alone." She shrugged. "Then this morning he told me he was sticking around and it was like he set off a bomb in my carefully constructed plan. I didn't react well, and he left, angry."

Green eyes studied her as Daisy listened to Sara's side of the story. "Tell me something. Why don't you want a relationship? Do you mean just with James or with any man?"

"Any man, really. My life is super busy. When would I have time to devote to a boyfriend?"

Daisy shrugged. "If it's the right man, it'll sort itself out."

"Yes, well, I'm not particularly fond of leading some poor guy on until I figure out if he's the right one. Which is what made James so perfect. I like him, but he's leaving. Or was supposed to be." She propped her elbows on the desk and covered her face with her hands. "Why did he have to change his mind?"

"I don't know, but you need to fix this. James likes you. He smiles whenever he talks about you. You've had him tied up in knots since he got here. Whether you want a relationship or not, you need to talk to him."

"I don't think we have any more to say to each other. We said it all before he left. He wants something long-term. I don't."

"Really? Don't think I haven't seen the way you look at Sloan when you hold him. Or the way you won't go out with me and Asa and Marci and Chet because you feel like the fifth wheel. Work isn't everything."

"Well, it's what I've got."

"Right. But what if you could have more?"

"Now you sound like James."

"Good." She stood. "Maybe you should think about it. I'm making myself a milkshake and leaving you to do just that." Pivoting with her cane, Daisy yanked open the door and left Sara to stare after her, thinking about what she said.

Sighing, she stared at the screensaver on her computer. This was precisely why she didn't want a man in her life. They mucked up everything.

Her body tingled as she remembered just how mucked up things got last night.

Maybe they didn't muck up *everything*.

Twenty

James hit save, then closed his laptop lid, looking out the window of his room. Gray clouds scuttled across the sky and a few fat snowflakes drifted toward the ground. It was supposed to snow again later.

The weather suited his mood. He'd been in a funk since his argument with Sara three days ago. One good thing had come of it: he'd written three more chapters since Saturday and outlined the rest of the novel, all of which he'd sent to Charlie. Every time he started to think about Sara—about what happened between them, good and bad—he'd pounded words out on the keyboard. He'd helped Asa in the barn too. Physical work was the only thing that really kept his mind off of her.

He stood, deciding he needed some of that again. Stretching his back, he laid the computer on the bed and went downstairs. Daisy sat on the living room couch, reading a book.

"Hey." She glanced up.

"Hey. I'm going to head out to the barn. Find some stalls to muck or something."

She nodded. "Asa's out there. They were inoculating some of the calves today."

"I'll see if they need another hand. Thanks."

"Yep."

He could feel her eyes on him as he walked out. Like she wanted to say something, but didn't have the courage. He wasn't about to ask her what it was. He already knew. Talking about Sara wasn't something he was ready to do. He'd bared his soul to that woman and all she could say was sorry.

Finding his boots and coat, he geared up and let himself out into the blustery wind. He could smell the snow coming and hoped it wouldn't knock out the power again. He wasn't ready for more cold showers and frigid nights by the fire.

Although, it wouldn't be like that here. The Stone Creek had the best generators on the market. There would be barely a blip in service. Maybe it would be a good thing. Then he wouldn't be tempted to drive to town to see Sara. It would save him from himself. He didn't know when he became such a glutton for punishment.

He snorted. Yes, he did. The first time he kissed her. He knew then he'd always want more.

Tugging on his insulated gloves, James veered toward the group of men in one of the side pastures. They had a smaller pen set up at one end full of young cattle. They filed through a narrow run into a chute at the end. Silas, having returned home yesterday, worked the rear gate while Asa was at the front. Jasper and another hand moved the cows through the run and another man James didn't recognize hung off the side of the chute, giving injections.

James climbed through the fence rails and jogged over to them. Asa glanced up.

"Dude, you look like shit."

"Thanks. I tried." He shrugged in a, "What can you do?"

gesture and offered his brother-in-law a tight smile. "Can I help?"

"Sure. Take over for Dad."

"What? I'm fine." Silas peered around the chute at James and Asa.

Asa snorted. "If you can take your glove off without wincing, I'll believe it."

"What's going on?" James asked.

"Nothing," Silas growled.

"Dad missed the timing to close the gate and the cow tried to back out. It stumbled forward, then it hit the gate. His hand was in the way and the gate slammed shut on it."

"It's fine." Silas gave Asa a fierce frown.

"Bullshit. You probably broke your finger. You're just scared to go in the house and tell Noreen."

"I'm not scared to tell her." Silas shifted. "I just don't want her to baby me. You know she will."

"Would that be so bad?"

Silas grumbled, making James laugh. "At least go in and get some ice on it or something. I'll take over." He studied the gate. "Though, after hearing your story, I'm not sure I want to."

"Ah, you'll be fine," Asa waved a hand. He released the calf in the chute. It bellowed and ran away toward the gate at the other end of the pasture. Another ranch hand swung the gate open to let it pass.

"Well, if you're going to do this, come here so I can show you how it's done." Silas waved James over. "Come around the front. You need to be on this side."

James ran around and let Silas show him what to do. It didn't appear too complicated.

And it wasn't, but he soon found out the cows were. They didn't like to cooperate. He understood how Silas crushed his fingers. He had a couple of narrow misses himself.

By the time he closed the last cow into the chute, he wasn't sure he'd have felt the gate closing on his hand anyway. His fingers were numb from the cold.

Asa released the cow and straightened, glancing back at the pen. "That the last one?"

James nodded.

"Awesome. Let's go get warm." Asa thanked the vet, then gathered up the rope they'd brought out to wrangle runaway cattle.

James followed him into the barn. Taking off his gloves, he flexed his fingers. "I don't know how you do this all day. I can't feel my hands."

"You need some of these." He took off one glove, then unzipped a pouch on the backside and pulled out a hand warmer.

"That would have been nice to know before I spent hours out there with you." He snatched the packet from Asa's fingers and flipped it over in his hand, feeling the warmth seep into his cold skin.

"Call it an initiation." Asa grinned. "Daisy would probably call it payback."

James chuckled. "Yeah. I probably deserve it." He would regret not sticking up for his sister for the rest of his life. But he was happy her rebellion landed her here with this man. She was where she was meant to be.

Asa let them into the office and took two bottles of water from the mini-fridge against the wall. He handed one to James, then rested a hip on the desk.

"Thanks." James twisted off the cap and took a drink. Despite the chill, the water felt good going down his throat. Who knew opening and closing a cattle chute in the cold could make him so thirsty?

"Yep." Asa took a swig of his own bottle. "So, I take it this was a distraction from Sara?"

Lowering the water bottle, James's expression turned dark. He'd managed to shove thoughts of her to the back of his mind while working. "I don't need a distraction from Sara."

"Mmm-hmm, sure. Look, take it from someone who's been a dumbass with a woman—go talk to her."

"It's not that simple. I thought we were building something, but she just wanted a quick fling. The only reason she went to bed with me was because she thought I was leaving. That we could just have one mind-blowing night and then part ways, happy that we shared what we did." He looked at the water bottle in his hand. "She doesn't want to talk to me. She wants me to leave so she can go back to her normal routine." He took another drink.

"You know, I've known Sara a long time. We were classmates. She's always been driven. To get good grades, good test scores. To get into the best colleges and have a solid plan for her future. She opened that diner at the age of twenty-three. When most other recent college graduates are fetching coffee and dry cleaning for their bosses, she *was* the boss."

James frowned. "Okay. What's your point?"

"My point is, I'm not sure Sara knows how to live her life any other way. She doesn't know how to slow down and take time for herself. She's never had a reason to. It's always been about succeeding."

"Which she's done in spades."

"Exactly. Maybe you're just what she needs to slow her down and get her to see that there's more to life than building a successful career or a successful business. Trust me, sometimes you need a smack upside the head to realize it. Don't give up on her, James. If you think there's something real there between you, don't give up. Not yet."

Asa stood and put a hand on James's shoulder. "I'm going to head inside. Think about what I said."

James nodded, already lost in his thoughts, as Asa left the

barn. Should he take Asa's advice and not give up? She hadn't seemed very open to a relationship the other day. Just apologetic that she'd hurt his feelings.

But what if Asa was right and she just didn't know how to live her life for herself? Was there enough of a spark to justify trying to convince her of that?

He scoffed as he turned to head back to the house. They damn near set the sheets on fire Friday night. There was plenty of spark. He just wasn't sure he wanted to put his heart on the line like that again. She could be completely aware she was missing out on something more and just didn't care. Maybe she'd judged a personal life as too much of a risk, and nothing anyone said or did would change her mind.

Was he ready to get rejected if that was the case?

Snow crunched under his boots as he left the barn. The cows they'd inoculated grazed on hay in the pasture. An occasional bellow reached his ears. A better question might be, could he go back to Chicago with no regrets if he didn't pursue her?

The churning in his gut told him the answer to that was no. He would always wonder "what if," if he didn't try again.

∽

Bone-weary after another long day, Sara stumbled through the door of her house. She was going to try the bath thing again tonight and hope no one interrupted her this time.

Like it was a bad interruption last time. Sara rolled her eyes at the sarcastic note to her thoughts. No, she had certainly enjoyed the interruption. And as much as her body wanted a repeat, it couldn't happen. James O'Malley didn't fit into her plans.

On her way to her bathroom, her brain registered the mess in her house. Dirty dishes sat in the sink, mail littered the counter, and a layer of dust coated most surfaces. She'd been so busy lately she hadn't cleaned much. Sighing, she pushed up her sleeves. It would drive her nuts if she didn't take care of some of this. She could at least do the dishes and sort the mail. Maybe take the duster to the floor. Mop near the door where she'd tracked in dirty snow and salt.

Sara moved to the sink and opened the dishwasher. A rack of dirty dishes greeted her, and she groaned. She never turned it on. Muttering a curse, she put a dishwasher tab in the dispenser and shut the door, pushing a couple of buttons. It kicked on, and she turned on the faucet and plugged the drain. She'd just wash the rest by hand. If she didn't do it tonight, she'd forget, and they'd sit there several more days.

She set her phone in the speaker dock on the counter and turned on some music, then squirted a dollop of dish soap into the water and started in on the pile of dishes. Humming along to the music, it didn't take her too long to wash them all. She dried her hands, then sorted the mail. Most of it was junk, but there were a couple of bills, and she filed them away to be paid later.

That done, she opened the tiny closet in the corner of the kitchen to get her floor duster and mop. Sorting through the cleaning supplies on the shelf, she tried to find the disposable cloths that went on the duster, but all she saw were mopping pads. "I really should invest in the reusable ones," she muttered. "Where the hell are they? I know I bought some." Finally, buried behind her sack of used grocery bags, she found the small box. "Gremlins. It was gremlins." Rolling her eyes, she took one out of the box and attached it to the duster.

She made quick work of the kitchen and moved out into the living room to get the areas around the rug. Her floral-patterned rug took up most of the space, so it only took her a few moments to walk the perimeter before she was moving on to the entryway.

The duster bumped the gift bag she dropped there Friday night. Her breath caught as she stared at it, memories flooding her head. Leaning the duster pole against the wall, she reached for the bag with a shaky hand. She reached inside and withdrew the toy. The plush fabric felt cool against her fingers.

"Dammit." James's face flashed in her mind, wearing that cocky smile while his blue eyes twinkled. Her heart lurched. She stuffed the toy back into the bag and marched into the kitchen, yanking open the trashcan drawer and throwing it in the bin.

Chest heaving, she stared at it, then growled. "Dammit!" She pulled the bag out and took the shark from the sack. Tossing the bag back in the trash, she kicked the drawer closed. "Damn man and his stupid nickname. I never asked to be called Shark. I never asked for you, either." She stared into the toy's beady eyes. "Didn't stop him, did it? Nope. He can't leave well enough alone. And now I'm talking to a fucking toy." She huffed and dropped her arm, still clutching the shark.

She glanced at it, trying to decide what to do with it. She couldn't throw it away. Marching down the hall to her room, she put it on her dresser. As much as she wanted to, she couldn't hate him or wish she'd never met him. Despite her initial assumptions about him, he was a nice man. A good man. Albeit a little cocky, but she didn't hold that against him. It was part of his charm. Which was why she now had a stuffed shark as a decoration.

Sara returned to the entryway and grabbed the duster pole, attacking the floors once more. She didn't know what to do about James. She thought she could walk away after one night. And if he'd left, she might have. It would have been a fond memory for her to look back on.

But now that he was sticking around for God only knew how long, she wasn't sure anymore. She just knew she wasn't interested in a long-distance thing. She wasn't even sure she was interested in a close distance thing. All she knew was he had her thinking about her priorities and whether she was wrong to exclude a serious relationship—with any man.

Pushing the pile of dust and debris into one spot, she retrieved the broom and swept it up. She dragged out the mop and quickly cleaned the kitchen floor and spot cleaned near the doors. Once she was satisfied the house was at least tidy, if not spic and span, she poured herself a glass of wine and retreated to her bathroom. She was going to let the hot water and wine wash away all thoughts of the blue-eyed devil that had turned her life topsy-turvy.

Twenty-One

Sara put her SUV in park as she stared at the main house on the Stone Creek. She hoped she wasn't making a mistake. But despite her best efforts, she couldn't shake thoughts of James from her mind. Even when she was asleep, he was there. In vivid detail. She woke up tangled in her sheets and panting this morning from the dreams she had of him. Her body heated just thinking about them.

So, here she was, getting ready to ask him if he wanted to spend the day with her. She was supposed to go to Billings with Daisy and Marci, but Sloan was sick, so they decided to reschedule. She could have gone to the diner and worked, but for once, she actually wanted a day off. Before she knew what she was truly thinking, she had her skis in the back and was on the road up here.

"Oh, just do it already." Yanking the door handle, she got out and climbed the steps to the front door. Asa knew she was here because he'd buzzed her through the front gate, so it wasn't like she could hide in her car or turn around and pretend she never arrived.

She wrapped her knuckles on the door once, only waiting a few moments before it opened.

"Hey, Sara. Daisy's in the kitchen." Asa stepped back to let her enter and motioned down the hallway.

"Actually, I'm not here to see Daisy. Is James around?"

The smile that spread over the man's face told her he knew all about their complicated relationship. "Yeah, he's upstairs. I'll go get him." He turned and ran up the stairs.

Not wanting to appear too eager, and because she wanted to say hello to Daisy, Sara wandered down the hall to the kitchen.

"Hey." Daisy glanced up as Sara entered. "What are you doing here?"

"I came to see if James wanted to go skiing. What are you making?"

"Gingerbread cookies. With as many people as I have to bake for this Christmas, I figured I'd better get started. I'll freeze them, then ice them closer to Christmas."

"Yum. I love gingerbread. I can't wait to taste yours."

"You can have one now, if you want." She pointed to the cookies cooling on wracks on the island. "I don't have any frosting, but they'll still taste good."

"Yeah, they will. You don't have to tell me twice." She hitched a hip on a bar stool and snatched a cookie, biting the head off the snowman.

"Hey! How come she gets a cookie and I got my fingers smacked with your spoon?"

Sara turned to see James and Asa in the doorway. James gave his sister a friendly glare.

Daisy smiled at him. "Because she didn't try to just take one. I offered."

"Even I've learned that, Jimmy." Asa patted James's shoulder and strode into the room to press a kiss to his wife's cheek.

Sara took pity on him and held up her half-eaten cookie. "Here. Take a bite."

He eyed her with a touch of surprise, but walked forward and leaned in to take a bite. His lips brushed her fingers as he closed his mouth around the gingerbread man's leg. A fine quake went through her as their eyes connected. He grasped her wrist to hold her hand steady. His thumb rubbed circles on the pulse point. Sara swallowed hard.

Asa cleared his throat. Sara jerked her wrist free and turned away. Oh, this was a bad idea. She should just go home. But the heat still flowing through her body wouldn't let her. Her need for the man short-circuited her brain. It screamed at her conscious mind to shut up and let her body take over.

As much as she wanted to, dragging James down to the kitchen floor and ravaging him wasn't something she could do in polite company.

"So, um, Asa said you came here to see me. What's up?"

She caught Daisy's smirk before she turned back to James and fought not to roll her eyes. At least someone saw the humor in all this. She took a deep breath and met his gaze. "I took the day off from the diner and decided to do some skiing. Would you like to join me?"

Shock made his eyes wide, but he quickly schooled his features into an unreadable mask. "What happened to we were just a fling?"

Asa coughed. "Dais, baby, can you help me with something? In the living room?" He wrapped an arm around her waist and guided her toward the door.

"Subtle, Ace. Subtle." She rolled her eyes at him, but went willingly.

Sara could have kissed him. She did not want an audience while she groveled.

James watched them leave, then looked at her. "Well?"

"I've had time to think. And yes, I did intend for us to be a onetime thing. I assumed you wanted the same thing, but you knew something I didn't: that you were staying. If we'd talked first, Friday night would have gone differently. I'd have thanked you for the toy, maybe offered you a cup of coffee, then you'd have left and we'd have both gone to bed alone."

"So, we never would have had sex if you'd known I was staying?"

She nodded. "Right."

"I'm confused. You didn't want a relationship then. Are you saying you do now? What changed?"

"Like I said, I've had a chance to think. I can't erase what happened. I don't want to. What I can do is deal with it and figure out what to do next."

He snorted. "Deal with it? I'm—we're—not some disease you just have to weather until you get to the other side."

"I know that. And that's not how I meant it." She huffed, looking away as she gathered her thoughts. "What I mean is that I need to accept that things are different. What we did—it changed everything. Not just our relationship. My entire world tipped on its axis. When you announced you were staying longer, I suddenly had to process that shift immediately. And it led me to realize something."

He arched an eyebrow. "Okay. So, that is what?"

Sara set her cookie down and fully faced him. Inhaling a deep breath, she held his gaze. "I need to change."

He straightened, listening. "Go on."

"What we shared—well, I've never experienced anything like it. I can't get it out of my head, even when I sleep. That's never happened to me before. I can't help but ask myself why that is."

A smug smile crossed his face. "I have some ideas."

His levity helped bolster her courage. One of her fears coming here was that he would snub her. After the way she acted, she wouldn't blame him if he did. But the look on his face now said he was open to hearing her out. She smiled at him. "I'm sure you do. I'm also sure they don't line up with the thoughts in my head. At least not entirely."

His grin grew, and he crossed his arms. "I'm listening."

"I guess what I'm saying is, can we try to see where this goes?"

Expression growing contemplative, he dropped his arms. "Why?"

She frowned, taken aback. "What do you mean, why? I just explained why."

"Not really. Basically, you said you want to try because the horse has left the barn and you got a thrill from it. That's not a valid enough reason for me. What do you want from this, Sara? Because I'm not looking for just a sex partner."

She made a disgusted sound deep in her throat. "God, you make it sound so tawdry. That's not what I want, either. Yes, the sex was great, but it's not why I can't get you out of my head. It's just what pushed you through the barriers I've put up. You're staying there all on your own." She sighed. "I like you. I think you're funny and smart and nice." His grin came back as she spoke, and she narrowed her eyes at him. "And cocky."

He laughed, making her smile too.

"And I've been thinking about something Daisy said to me. I told her I had enough in my life with work and my friends, but she asked me what if I could have more? I've never wanted more until you came along."

He studied her for another moment. "Are you sure about this? I meant what I said, Sara. I'm not in this for anything less than forever. If that's not what you're hoping this could be, too, then let's just agree that the sex was fun, but we're just going to be friends."

Her heartbeat sped up as a thrill went up her spine at the thought of being James's forever. A thrill and just a hint of fear. If this didn't work out, it would take her a long time to pick up all the pieces of her heart. But she owed it to herself to try. No other man had ever occupied the places James did. Not even come close. And she was ready for more to her life than her diner and her friends.

"I'm sure." She held his gaze, not wanting him to doubt her sincerity.

His deep blue eyes bore into hers. Sara got the feeling they could see her soul. Hell, he probably could. James could read her better than anyone else ever had.

He finally gave a quick nod. "Okay."

"Okay?" She straightened, shifting her feet as hope lit in her chest.

"Yes. Let's give this a shot."

Nerves of a different sort fluttered in Sara's belly. She hadn't had a boyfriend since high school. There had been men, but never anything serious or official since her teens.

But a sense of rightness helped calm her fears. She wanted this. Life with James seemed brighter than life without him.

"Okay." She smiled up at him.

He leaned down and pressed a soft kiss to her lips. She curled her hands into his shirt, wishing they weren't standing in the Stone Creek's kitchen.

James lifted his head to smile at her. "So, skiing, huh?"

She smiled back and nodded. "Yeah. I haven't been in a while and it sounded fun."

"You might rethink that once you get out there with me. I've never skied."

Her eyes widened. "Never?" She found that hard to believe. James had the build of a natural athlete.

He shook his head. "Nope. Not many ski slopes in Chicago, and I'm not normally a cold-weather vacation type of person. I prefer the beach. I've water skied, though, so I'm guessing I shouldn't have too much trouble picking it up."

Sara shrugged. "Maybe. I guess we'll find out."

"Yep. I'm going to go change. Do I need to see if Asa has skis I can borrow?" He frowned. "I doubt any ski boots he has will fit me, though. His feet are bigger than mine."

"No. We're going up to the resort. They have rentals. We'll get you some gear there. You might want to borrow his ski goggles, though, or bring some sunglasses." It was chilly today, but the sun shone bright. Being on the slopes would be blinding.

He nodded. "I'll be back in a few minutes."

She returned his nod and sat down at the island, picking up her cookie to finish it. Anticipation swirled in her belly now, replacing the nerves. Some of her doubts about if this was the right thing were gone after their conversation. Now she was excited to see where this led. There was still a small part of her that hoped Daisy was right and that going after more was worth the risk to her heart.

Twenty-Two

Snow puffed around James, landing on his head and shoulders in a fine mist as he landed on his ass once again. Sara's laughter echoed off the mountainside. He growled and struggled to his feet. "This is ridiculous. I shouldn't be having this much trouble."

She skied to a stop beside him. "I told you it's not the same as water skis. You're standing too straight. Bend your knees more and center yourself over your feet. You'll get it."

He grumbled and looked down the bunny slope. A five-year-old whizzed by him, looking like a pro. Dammit. If a child could do this, so could he. Lifting his knees like she showed him, he turned to point the tips of his skis downhill. Using his poles, he pushed off again.

A shriek from behind drew his attention. He turned in time to see a little girl about seven sailing toward him. Her arms flailed wildly. He could hear who he assumed was her dad yelling for her to sit down, but her wide eyes told James she couldn't hear anything except the thud of her own heart. His instincts kicked in and he turned, spinning around to face her just as she reached him. He shot a hand out and snagged her waist, pulling her into him as he went down onto his butt in the snow.

"Are you okay?" He looked down at the girl's flushed face. She stared up at him with wide brown eyes.

"Yeah."

"Ava!" The man who'd been yelling a moment ago skied to a stop beside them. "Oh my gosh, honey, are you okay?"

"I'm fine, Daddy. Can we go get hot chocolate now?"

The man nodded. "Yeah. I think that sounds like a good idea." He glanced at James. "Thanks for stopping her."

"No problem." He helped her up just as Sara reached them.

"You guys okay?"

"Yeah, we're fine." He stared up at her from his seat in the snow. "I like her idea of hot chocolate, though. Maybe after a break we can come back out with me on a snowboard." He'd picked the skis, thinking they would be easiest since he could water ski, but now he was thinking he'd like to have his feet locked together.

"If that's what you want to do. I think if you try again now, though, you'll find you do fine so long as you stay out of your head. When you saw that girl in trouble, you reacted instinctively and swiveled like a pro."

He shrugged. "I still want hot chocolate."

She giggled. "Okay. Come on." She offered him a hand, and he used it to balance himself as he got to his feet.

"Ready?" she asked.

"Yeah. Let's do this." He eyed the rest of the bunny slope, wondering if he could indeed make it to the bottom without landing on his ass again.

"Remember, stay out of your head."

"Right." He sighed. "Let's go." This time when he pushed off, he stopped trying to concentrate on his skis and just let his body feel the mountain. She was right. He'd been trying too hard. It's what he should have done all along. The differences from water skiing had been enough to throw him, and he hadn't adjusted.

They reached the bottom, and he swung sideways, spraying snow as he stopped.

"See! I told you!" Sara lifted her goggles, grinning at him.

He laughed. "You did."

"You still want to switch to a snowboard?"

"I think so, yes. It'll be more like surfing, and I'm a better surfer than water skier."

She nodded once. "Okay. Let's go get our hot chocolate and find you a snowboard." Using her pole, she unlocked her boots from the skis. James did the same, and they headed inside.

Warm air heated his chilled cheeks as they stepped into the lodge. He lifted his goggles and tugged off his gloves, stowing the latter in his pockets. He took out his phone from his inner jacket pocket to check the time and saw he'd missed a call from his agent, Charlie. She hadn't left a message, but there was a text asking him to call.

"Hey, can you get our hot chocolate? My agent called, and I need to call her back." He'd sent her the first seven chapters of his book yesterday, so he imagined she had some thoughts on them.

Sara nodded. "I'll find us a table if you're not back before it's ready."

"Sounds good." He smiled and walked toward the fringes of the room, where it was quieter. Dialing Charlie's number, he waited for her to answer.

"Charlie Mills."

"Hey, Charlie. It's James."

"Hi. I wondered if you'd call me back."

With a frown, he glanced out the window at the ski slopes. "Why wouldn't I?"

"Because this book—it's not what we discussed."

"I know. But it's not that far off. It's still a spy novel."

"About a psychopath."

"Who's being hunted by a spy."

She sighed. "Why did you go this route?"

"Because I couldn't get behind the character I had. He was boring. I mean, how many spy series are there? Too many. This one has a twist. He'll be the villain people hate to love."

She sighed again, and he could imagine her leaning back in her desk chair, rolling her eyes at him. It made him grin. "Is that your only objection to the chapters I sent you?"

"Is it—? It's a pretty big thing to object to, James."

"Well, you're going to have to get used to it, because I have the whole thing mapped out, as well as the next couple of books. Plus, I don't have time to rewrite it if you want me to meet my deadline."

Charlie growled. "Did you do this to purposely piss me off?"

He snorted. "No. I did it because it was the story rattling around in my head that fit the spy narrative you and the publisher want me to write. Look, it will be fine. I think it's just what the spy world needs."

"Yeah, but, James, spy novels are supposed to have a hero people can get behind."

"It will, but it's going to make people uncomfortable while they do. Fascinated and uncomfortable."

"You make me hate my job, you know that, right?"

He laughed. "Yep. Hey, I have to go, but I'll send you some more chapters later this week."

"Yeah, okay. Talk to you soon."

"Yep. Bye." She echoed him, and he hung up. Sliding the phone back into his jacket, he found Sara at a table.

"Everything okay?"

He nodded and sat down. Picking up the cup in front of

him, he took a sip. "So, this is the resort your dad managed?" He glanced around the interior of the lodge. Giant crystal chandeliers hung from the high ceilings, reflecting off the tall windows. The walls were pine logs, cut by river rock fireplaces on either end of the room. Sound echoed through the cavernous space, but it wasn't overwhelming. Plush furnishings and drapes helped to dampen the noise.

"Yeah. It still looks the same, but different. They updated the upholstery. Added the coffee shop." She gestured to the small café set along the back wall.

"Is being a resort manager's daughter how you got so good at skiing?"

She nodded. "I spent almost as much time on the slopes as the ski patrol."

"Did you ever consider skiing as a profession?"

She wavered a hand. "For a couple of years, yeah. But I took a nasty fall when I was sixteen doing a practice slalom run. Broke my leg, gave myself a concussion. It wasn't the first spill I'd taken, but it was the most serious. I got back on my skis once my leg healed, but my heart wasn't in it anymore. I didn't have that drive to compete." She sipped her hot cocoa.

"Why a restaurant?"

"I like to cook. And bake. Other than skiing, it was the only thing that made sense to me."

"So, what's your degree in, then? Hospitality management?"

She shook her head. "Business. I worked in the resort restaurant through my teens, so I knew how one ran. I just wanted the business acumen to run my own." She studied him over the rim of her cup. "Daisy said you never wanted to be a lawyer. That your brothers pressured you into it. That true?"

"Sort of. There was nothing wrong with the idea. But yeah, I always just wanted to be a writer. In the end, Ian was right. I needed something to finance my dream and give me a better skill set to do it." He held up a hand. "But don't tell him I said that. It would feed his ego." He laughed.

She grinned. "So, you wouldn't change it?"

James looked over at the other patrons as he contemplated her question. Would he? He didn't regret it. "I'm not sure. Probably not. The way I look at it, I wouldn't be where I am if I'd walked a different path." His eyes found hers. "And that includes you."

Sara blushed. He should play Prince Charming in an adaptation of "Cinderella." He was a natural. She tipped her cup up, hiding her blush. "You about ready to strap on that snowboard?"

Taking a hearty swig of his hot chocolate, he nodded. "Bring it. I want one run down the bunny slope to make sure I'm not going to face plant and get run over by better skiers, then I want to take the lift to an actual slope. I'm done playing."

She laughed. "I hope you're better at it than skiing or it won't matter how many times you do the bunny slope."

"Oh, I will be. I think I have it figured out now."

She lifted an eyebrow. "Really? We'll see." Scooting her chair back, she stood, hot cocoa in hand. "Let's go."

Sara glanced at James from the corner of her eye as they made their way through the lodge to the rental office. He looked eager to try snowboarding. She was glad. She was having fun and didn't want to leave yet.

As they reached the rental office, they finished their hot cocoa and tossed the cups into a trash can. Inside, James exchanged his skis for a snowboard and they headed outside to take the escalator to the top of the bunny slope.

James snapped his boots into the buckles on the board while the instructor manning the slope gave him some pointers. Sara was sure he hadn't heard a one, because all his attention was on the slope and not the instructor. But when he pushed off and started down the hill, she realized he heard every word. Now she could see the natural athlete in him. His stance on the board was perfect as he glided down the hill. She took off after him.

Snow sprayed as she came to a halt. Lifting her goggles, she met his grin. "You did great."

"Thanks. That was a lot more fun than skis. Have you ever tried it?"

She nodded. "Yes, but I prefer skis. I've just spent more time on them, so they're what I'm comfortable with."

"That's reasonable." He leaned down and unbuckled his boots from the board. "Come on. Let's go catch that lift."

"You sure you don't want to practice more?"

He shook his head. "No, I'm good."

"Okay, but please don't go all cowboy on me. I don't want to explain to Daisy why I brought you back broken."

He laughed. "Deal."

They made their way to the line for the ski lift. As they got closer to the chairs, James strapped the board to his feet again and let Sara tow him forward.

"You know, most snowboarders just hop."

He grinned. "Where's the fun in that?"

She rolled her eyes and shoved him forward. "Get in the chair."

James waggled his eyebrows. "That sounds kinky."

"Kinked is exactly what you're going to be if you miss that chair and go tumbling." She bit back a laugh.

"Yeah, yeah." He hopped forward, waiting for the chairlift to come around. It whisked in behind them and lifted them off their feet.

Sara settled deeper into the seat and looked around. It had been far too long since she skied. "Thanks for coming with me. This is fun."

He smiled. "It is. I'm glad we cleared the air. I'm sorry we didn't before we slept together, but I'm glad it's worked out."

"Me too." She leaned into his shoulder and enjoyed the view. She felt him press a long kiss to the top of her head.

The lift reached the top, and they pushed off the chair, coasting away to find the correct slope. Sara could go down any of them, but she wanted an easier one for James. She was sure he'd try a harder slope, but she meant what she said. She didn't want to break him.

"Which way?"

She pointed toward a trail marked with a green piste marker. "Let's try that one. If you do well, we'll go down a blue run the next time."

"Works for me. Last one down buys the next round of hot chocolate." He flashed her a grin, then hopped forward and leaned into the hill, letting gravity pull him down the slope.

"Hey! Cheater!" She pushed off with her poles and skis, then tucked the poles into her sides and crouched, gaining speed to catch up with him.

She'd already planned to give him a head start, but he didn't know that. Grinning as she passed him, she sailed around some slower skiers and reached the bottom, slowing with a wide spray of snow. She glanced back to see James not far behind. He grinned as he used the edge of his board to slow, having figured out the mechanics. What he didn't figure on was the ice embedded in the powder. His board hit a ridge and caught, sending him tumbling forward.

Sara's laughter rang out as he landed on his face at her feet. He groaned as he pushed to his hands and knees. Tears streamed down her face as she doubled over.

"Oh, it's that funny, huh?"

She nodded, swiping at her face. Her laugh turned to a shriek as he tackled her into the snow. A handful of the cold crystals landed on her face, falling down into her collar. Squeals competed with more laughs as she tried to wiggle away. Finally, he used his size to trap her beneath him, holding her hands above her head.

"Do you give up?"

Giggling, she shook her head.

More snow went down her collar, making her gasp.

"How about now?" He rolled at the waist, so she was on top. The melting snow slid down inside her shirt to run down between her breasts. She sucked in a breath as the icy water hit her sensitive skin.

"Oh, you're going to pay," she breathed.

"Really?" His smile turned wicked. "I can't wait." Lifting his head, he kissed her.

Sara forgot the cold as he warmed her body with his touch. She forgot where they were until a vibration under her chest drew her attention. "What is that?"

"What's what?" He frowned, then glanced away, sitting up. "Wait. That's my phone." He unzipped his jacket and pulled it out just as it stopped ringing. "It's Daisy." He hit the button to call her back and put it on speaker. She answered on the first ring.

"Oh my God, you need to get back here."

"What?" He shared a look with Sara. "Why? Is everyone okay?"

"We are, yes. But the sheriff just called. They found another body."

Twenty-Three

Sara turned into the ranch drive and punched in the code James rattled off. The gates parted, and she drove through. As they neared the house, the flashing blue and red strobes of police cars came into view.

"How did the killer get onto the ranch?" Sara wondered aloud.

"It's thousands of acres, and there are access roads all over the place. He could have driven up one and carried the body over the property line."

"But why? Why dump the body here?"

"Notoriety, maybe? It's sure to make the news that a murder victim was found on Asa Mitchell's ranch."

He had a point. But the guy could have accomplished the same level of notoriety by dumping the body somewhere public. It might not have been as sensational, but after Hunter Goodman's murder, the national news outlets would have picked up the story of a second, publicly dumped murder victim in Asa Mitchell's hometown.

She pulled up in front of the garage, and they climbed out,

going inside. Several heads turned toward them, including the sheriff.

Sara's gaze roved over the group, pausing on Daisy, whose eyes were red-rimmed. "Daisy? Have you been crying?"

James stiffened beside her. "What's going on? Who was killed?"

Asa turned shell-shocked eyes on them. "One of the ranch hands. Benny. Jasper found him while he was out checking the herd in the back pastures."

"Oh my God," Sara breathed. "What happened?"

Asa swallowed hard. Daisy choked on a sob. So did Nori. Silas ran a hand down her back.

"He was stabbed," the sheriff said. "Multiple times. And carved."

"Carved?" Alarm made James's voice sharp.

Katy nodded. "Carved." She took a steadying breath. "When was the last time either of you saw Benny? We're trying to establish a timeline. Asa said he didn't show up to work yesterday or today."

"I'm not sure," Sara hedged. She searched her memory, trying to think of the last time he was in the diner. "He usually comes in on the weekends because he comes into town to go to the bar with his friends. I don't remember seeing him this weekend, though."

James held up his hands. "I don't even know which ranch hand we're talking about."

Asa took out his phone and scrolled, showing James a picture. Sara's heart ached at the sight of the smiling, dark-haired, brown-eyed man leaning against a fence post as he held up a new hat.

"I think I saw him in the barn last week." James studied the picture, then focused on Katy. "Wednesday, maybe."

She nodded. "That fits with what everyone else has said so

far. They had the weekend off for the holiday, so no one's seen him since Wednesday."

"Do you know how long he's been—" James rolled his hand and glanced at his sister. She stood with one arm wrapped around her middle and the other bent, covering her mouth with her hand.

Katy's mouth flattened. "Not yet, no. Jasper was pretty shaken up, and I haven't been out there yet."

"Did you look into Jeffries?"

"Jeffries?" Sara turned to look at him. "You still think he's up to something?" She shook her head. "I'm telling you, you're wrong." She agreed he was odd—withdrawn—but not that he was dangerous. He never made her nervous until after James planted the seed that he could be bad news.

"I wouldn't be so sure." Katy smoothed a hand down her long blonde ponytail and flipped it over her shoulder. "I dug a little deeper into his background. Billy Jeffries didn't exist until twenty-five years ago."

"What? How is that possible?" Silas asked. "He's in his forties."

Katy nodded. "I'm guessing he changed his name, but from what, I don't know. I need his fingerprints to look for an ID."

"The boxes. At the church from the Thanksgiving dinner. He helped me bring them in." Sara glanced at James, then Katy.

The sheriff's mouth twisted. "We can try, but cardboard is hard to get prints off of."

"Some of the boxes were glossy. I think Cynthia saved them. She talked about reusing them for the food pantry. And they didn't have their normal hours this weekend because of the holiday," Sara added. "They're probably all still piled up in the kitchen or the pantry room."

Katy pulled out her phone. "I'll send a deputy down there

to collect them. Can you meet him there to show him which ones?"

"Of course."

"Perfect." Katy lifted the phone to her ear.

"Come on," James said. "I'll go with you."

They hurried from the house and out to Sara's car, not wanting to keep the deputy waiting any longer than necessary. Sara might have sped a little on the way to town, but tried to keep it to a minimum. Veering off the road into a ravine wouldn't help matters, and it wasn't like the boxes were going to get up and walk away before they could get to the church.

Sara's hands shook as she pulled into the parking lot. Her eyes went to the dumpster. The yellow crime scene tape had been removed, but she could still see the scene as it was Thursday afternoon. Hunter's pale face and unseeing eyes entered her mind, and she swallowed hard, forcing herself to look away from where she found his body.

A large masculine hand wrapped around hers on the steering wheel. She glanced at James.

"You okay?"

She offered him a tremulous smile. "Yeah. I'll be fine." She pulled on the door handle. "Let's go find those boxes." Stepping out of the vehicle, she rounded the hood and met the deputy, who climbed out of his car carrying a small black case. She still couldn't see Billy as the killer, but she understood the police needed to follow every lead, and even she had to agree it was strange that a man in his forties had only existed on paper for twenty-some years.

"I'm Deputy Scanlon." The fresh-faced blonde man held out a hand, turning curious eyes on James.

"James O'Malley." James shook his hand. "This is Sara Katsaros."

The man smiled. "I know. Best pie around." He sobered

and his eyes widened. "Don't tell Chief Deputy Hughes I said that. If he told his mom, she'd skin me alive."

Sara laughed. "Cynthia?"

He blushed and nodded.

"Your secret's safe with us. Come on. Let's get those boxes." She led them inside, flipping on lights as they moved toward the kitchen. She hadn't paid too much attention to where the boxes went when they were unloaded, but she was pretty sure she remembered seeing a stack in the back of the kitchen. The rest would have made it into the food pantry area to be used by patrons.

"There." She pointed to the stack in the corner by the coat rack.

Deputy Scanlon set the case he carried on one of the long prep tables and opened it. He put on a pair of purple nitrile gloves, then picked up a container of black powder and a brush.

"Can we help?" James asked.

"Uh, sure. Grab some gloves. You can line the boxes up on the tables, and I'll come down the row and dust them."

Sara and James both covered their hands, then went to work.

"I'm going to look in the pantry area. There were more than this." She wandered down the hall to the food pantry, finding the rest of the boxes she brought the other day stacked near the front desk where patrons checked in and out. Being careful not to smudge any visible prints, she took the boxes back to the kitchen and lined them up with the others.

"Deputy, why don't you start lifting the ones you found and let us dust?"

Scanlon straightened. "Sure." He held out the brush and powder.

James took the items and continued where he left off. Sara

followed Scanlon as he lifted prints, taking the cards from him as they went.

Sara's hands sweat and itched inside the gloves by the time they finished. She peeled them off and tossed them in the trash as Scanlon stowed all the cards in an evidence bag and latched his kit.

"That's it. I'll get these to the lab to be run. Hopefully, we know something soon."

Sara agreed, troubled by the gruesome events gripping her town. Stuff like this didn't happen here.

"Thanks, deputy." James put a hand on her back, ushering her outside.

Scanlon waved and climbed into his car.

"Now what?" Sara looked up at James.

He shrugged. "We wait."

Twenty-Four

Lost in thought, James was pulled back to the present when Sara turned off the main road on their way back to the Stone Creek. He glanced around to realize they were on the road to her house. "Sara?"

She turned tired eyes on him. "I hope you don't mind. I don't really want to be alone."

He could see in her eyes and by the lines on her face that thoughts of what had occurred in the last few days weighed heavily on her. "I don't mind. I don't want you to be alone, either."

With a curt nod, she returned her attention to the road, and they soon pulled into the driveway of her white ranch-style home.

Parking the car in the garage, the door whirred as James got out. The thud of the car doors shutting echoed off the concrete floor. Sara let them inside, setting her purse on the counter and draping her coat over a bar stool.

"What do you want for dinner?" She glanced at him over her shoulder as she walked to the fridge.

"You don't have to cook. I can make myself a sandwich."

"It'll help keep my mind off things. What do you want?"

He shrugged. "Whatever you want to make. I'm not picky."

She nodded and opened the freezer door. "How about chicken-fried steak and green bean casserole?"

"Sure. Sounds great. Can I help with anything?"

"No. Not in here. You could start a fire, though."

He nodded once. "Of course." After taking off his coat and boots, James wandered into the living room and laid kindling in the fire grate. It didn't take him long to have flames crackling. A glance into the kitchen showed him Sara hard at work making dinner. Her shoulders were tense and her brow pinched like she had a headache. He had an idea of how he could alleviate some of the tension, but he wasn't sure she'd go for it.

Backing away, he headed down the hall to the bathroom. It was better to ask forgiveness than permission in this case. He turned on the faucet in the bathtub and plugged the drain. She was going to soak in there for at least a few minutes, even if he had to pry the cooking utensils from her fingers.

James rummaged through the cabinet in the corner, looking for her bath stuff, and found a lavender bath bomb. He dropped it into the hot water, then headed back to the kitchen.

She looked up from stirring a pot as he entered. "Hey. Dinner isn't quite ready yet. The casserole has to cook." She pointed to the glass pan sitting on the counter containing the green bean casserole. The oven beeped, and she paused her stirring to put the dish in the oven.

"How long does that have to cook?"

"Half an hour or so. I already put the chicken in. I just need to finish this gravy, but that should only take a couple more minutes."

"Good." He leaned against the wall to wait. When she

shut off the heat and moved the pan off the burner and put a lid on it, he walked forward and took her hands.

"What are you doing?"

"Come with me."

"Why?"

"Because you need to relax. You're stiff as a board."

"James—"

He shook a finger at her. "No. No arguing. Come on."

She huffed, but let him pull her out of the kitchen and down the hall. "What's this?"

James reached over and shut off the water. "You're going to climb into that tub and relax for a little while."

"But dinner—"

"Is mostly finished. I can take the food out if you're worried about it. Now, strip."

She arched a brow at him.

"Please?"

A smile teased her lips at his boyish plea. "Fine. But if you burn dinner, I'm going to be really pissed. I don't want to eat a sandwich. Not after today."

"Eagle Scout, remember? I aced the cooking badge."

She chuckled. "Okay."

He backed toward the door. "I'll leave you be. If I watch you undress, dinner will definitely burn."

A blush stained her cheeks, and she bit her lip. James stifled a groan and backed out of the room. The temptation to join her was strong, but now wasn't the time. She needed to relax first. And they needed to talk about how they wanted this relationship to proceed before they did anything.

He busied himself around the house while he waited for the food to finish, tidying up the kitchen and hanging up their coats. Just as the timer went off on the oven, Sara appeared, dressed in light blue sweatpants and a long-sleeved gray t-shirt. Part of him was glad she skipped the robe. If he had to sit with her while she wore it, he'd never be able to concentrate on their conversation.

"You cleaned." She crossed the kitchen and picked up the hot pads next to the stove and opened the oven. "You didn't have to do that."

"I'm eating too. It didn't seem right for you to do all the work." He took some plates from the cupboard and laid them on the counter.

Sara set the casserole and the steak on the stove and picked up a spatula. "Well, I appreciate it. Are you ready to eat?"

He nodded. "I'm starving. Skiing worked up my appetite. It died when we learned about Benny, but it's come back now that I smell food."

"Yeah, me too." She lifted the steaks from the pan and put them on the plates. Finding a ladle, she spooned gravy over them, then dished out the green bean casserole. "I wish we still had some pie."

"Me too."

"I can make cookies after we eat." She glanced at him. "I have some dough in the freezer."

"Cookies sound good." He took two forks from the silverware drawer and handed her one. She took it and passed him a plate.

"Do you want to eat at the table or by the fire?"

"Fire." He wasn't really cold, but the flames would be comforting.

They took their plates into the living room and settled into the same places they sat the last time: James on the couch, and Sara in the chair.

For several minutes, they didn't talk, both too hungry to do more than fill their bellies. Once the edge was gone, James looked up from his plate to study her.

"Why are you staring at me?" She lifted a bite of green beans to her mouth.

It took James a moment to register her question. She said it so casually. He inhaled a breath. "We need to talk."

"Uh-oh. Those words are never a good way to start a conversation."

He smiled. "Depends on how you look at it. I think we need to talk about us."

She frowned. "What about us?"

"Where do you see this going?"

"This? You mean you and me?"

He nodded.

She blew out a breath and pushed her food around with her fork. "I'm not sure. We've sort of talked about this already. Forever, remember?"

James tipped his head. "Yeah, but what does that look like? We said we'd try and see where this went, but we didn't talk about where we actually wanted it to go."

"Doesn't that imply that we want it to work and to stay together?"

"Yes, but as what? Long-term lovers? Husband and wife?"

Her eyes widened. "You want to get married?"

"Eventually, that would be the goal, yes. But first we have to tackle the fact that we live twelve hundred miles apart."

She glanced down at her plate. "That was one of my reasons for not wanting more than one night." She looked up. "I don't want a long-distance relationship."

"I don't either."

"So, where does that leave us?"

"With one of us moving." He took a deep breath and said what was rattling around in his head. "My career is easy to pick up and move, so that would be me."

Her eyes grew wide again. "You'd uproot your whole life for me?"

"Well, yeah." He glanced at the fire, gathering his thoughts. "I want us to work, Sara." His gaze returned to hers.

"I've never met anyone like you. Never felt this way about a woman. If we stand a chance, I think I need to be here."

Her fork clattered against her plate as she put it down with a shaky hand. "I agree we need to be in the same place, but I don't want you to give up your life for me. I don't want you to come to resent me for having to move here."

James frowned. "Why would I resent you? This was my idea."

She rolled her lips in and turned to look at the fire. "I just don't want to feel like a burden."

"Honey—" James set his plate down and crossed to crouch in front of her, taking her hands. "Where is this coming from?"

Tears pooled in her eyes, and she sniffed. "You know how I said my parents moved back to New Mexico when the resort closed?"

He nodded.

"I overheard them talking one day shortly before they left. Dad was saying how glad he was that they could finally go home. Mom agreed, but said she was glad they'd stayed for me. For *me*. Then she said she was glad he turned down the position in Ruidoso a couple of years before so I could stay in the same school. That she knew he hated working for the resort here, but was proud that he stayed." She sniffed again. "He hated it here. They both did. They couldn't stand the weather. All their friends and family were in New Mexico. But they stayed because I liked my school. Do you have any idea how that made me feel? To know my parents were miserable because of me?"

James squeezed her hands. "Honey, they did it because they love you. And I'm betting they don't resent you, do they?"

She frowned. "No."

"So why are you worried they do?"

Her frown deepened.

"Guilt can make a person miserable. Especially when there's no reason to feel guilty. You didn't force your parents to stay. They did it because they wanted to make you happy, not because you asked. The same thing goes for us. You're not asking me to move here. I'm volunteering. And I can guarantee I will never resent you because I moved here for us. You might hear me complain about the snow and the cold—in fact, I guarantee you will—but I will never resent you for it. If, for some reason, we don't work out and I want to, I'll move back to Chicago. But you are worth more than any city or apartment to me. Just like you are to your mom and dad." He wrapped a hand around the back of her neck and pressed his forehead to hers. "Okay?"

She drew in a shaky breath and nodded. "Okay."

He placed a gentle kiss on her mouth. "How about we finish our dinner and then I show you just how happy I am to be here?"

A giggle slid past her lips. "Can it involve strip poker?"

James laughed. "Eager to show off your poker skills? I have to warn you. I'm better at poker than Uno."

She grinned. "No. I just want to make sure I'm worthy of my new shark friend. Can't disappoint Killer."

Another laugh boomed from James's chest. "I'm sure he'll be delighted with your performance."

Twenty-Five

James whistled as he strode down the sidewalk. He'd come into town to eat lunch with Sara, then decided to go for a walk before heading back to her house to write some more. The last couple of days had been pure bliss. Almost too good to be true, in fact. He kept waiting for something to happen and tear the rug out from under him. Changing Sara's mind about a relationship had been easy. Too easy. She'd either been ready to move to a new chapter in her life or she was putting on a good show—for both of them.

He hoped it wasn't the latter. He didn't want to think she was deluding herself into being happy with him.

Across the street, he spotted the sheriff climb from her cruiser and head toward the police station. Curious about whether she'd heard anything back on the prints Deputy Scanlon took from the church, he called out to her and jogged across the road.

"James, hi." She smiled at him, her honey-colored eyes twinkling gold in the bright sunshine.

He returned her smile. "Hi. So, I was wondering if you

had any more leads on Benny's case. I haven't been up to the ranch much in the last couple of days to talk to anyone."

She frowned. "Aren't you staying there?"

"I was, but I've sort of moved in with Sara."

Katy's face brightened. "Good for you. And her. I'm glad. She's a nice person."

"Thanks."

She nodded once, then motioned him to follow her. "I could use a sounding board. This case is bizarre, and my deputies and I don't know what to make of it." She led him into the building. He signed in, then followed her to her office.

"Have a seat."

He sank into the guest chair while she moved around behind her desk. "What have you learned?"

She folded her hands on the desk. "Most of the prints belonged to church members or the people who donated the items, but I got a hit back on Billy's prints. They matched the ones on his military record. But they also matched those in a sealed file from twenty-five years ago."

"Sealed? Was it a juvenile record?"

She shook her head. "No, but that would have made sense. Billy's forty-two. He'd have been seventeen then. It was a name change case in Bennettsville, Georgia, but the record was sealed at the time of the change. The record didn't mention his current or former name, but the prints were linked to the file."

"Courts only do that if there's a danger to the person changing their name."

"Yep. I put in a request to have it unsealed, but without any evidence linking him to either murder, I'm not holding my breath. I wrote in the request that Jeffries is missing—which is true. We haven't been able to locate him. So, I'm hoping the Georgia courts take that into account. I doubt his disappearance is related to whatever caused him to change his name, but you never know."

James propped an elbow on the chair arm and ran a finger over his top lip, staring at a point past her shoulder. "Let me do some digging. I know a prosecutor in Atlanta. A buddy of mine from law school. He's a native Georgian. He might know something or be able to point me toward some news sources from that time period. If it was anything major that caused him to change his name, there's probably a record of it somewhere."

She held up her hands. "I will not argue if you want to take on that task."

"Good, because I really don't mind. It'll give me a break from writing when I need one, plus it frees up your deputies for other things." He dropped his hand. "Do you have any other leads? Any suspects? In either murder?"

Her expression darkened. "No. No one saw anything or heard anything. Once Jasper collected himself, he did what he does best and tried to track how Benny got there, but he didn't get very far. Any tracks leading to Benny's body were obliterated by cattle and other wildlife. I even brought in our K-9, but he didn't have any luck either. I don't even have a definitive cause of death. The M.E. said he thinks he was stabbed, but there's too much predation to confirm it; the wildlife did a number on his body. All we do know is that whoever did it is a sick, twisted individual. Those symbols carved into his body weren't self-inflicted. Most of them were post-mortem."

"What kind of symbols?"

She shrugged. "Can't tell for sure. They look like a series of lines, but so far, forensics hasn't been able to identify them."

"Do you have pictures of the symbols? I've researched

cryptography extensively for my novels. Maybe I can make sense of it."

She hesitated. "I'm not sure..." Her voice trailed off, and she bit her lip.

"If you're worried about how I'll react to the crime scene photos, don't. I was a prosecuting attorney for the city of Chicago. I've seen murder victims before."

She blew out a breath, widening her eyes. "Not like this. But okay. We're at a standstill and I'm short-handed, so congratulations, you're officially a consultant for the Campbell County Sheriff's Department." She opened a file folder on her desk and rifled through it, pulling out a stack of photos to slide them across the desk.

James picked them up. He dug deep for the detached prosecutor he used to be and studied the photographs. "They look like runes." He glanced up at Katy. "Why would someone carve runes into a body?" Something niggled in the back of his mind. He couldn't put his finger on it, but something about the runes bothered him.

She shrugged. "I have no idea."

"Anyone around here into that sort of thing? Viking or Bronze Age history?"

"No one comes to mind. We have a few locals who look like Vikings, but whether they're obsessed with the culture, I don't know." She tipped a finger to the pictures. "You really think those are Viking runes?"

"Or some other ancient language, yes. I don't know what they mean, though. Can you make me copies of just the symbols? I know a language database I can run them through. Maybe I can piece together what they say."

"Sure."

He handed her back the pictures, and she spun around to the all-in-one printer combo behind her. Once she copied the ones with symbols, she handed him the papers, then put the original photographs back in the file.

"Tell me if I'm crazy here, but is this a serial killer?"

His mouth flattened. That uneasy feeling he had about the runes gripping him again. "I don't know. But I think the sooner we figure out what these mean, the better. It might give us a clue as to who's behind this." He stood.

Katy rose and stretched a hand over her desk. "Thanks, James. I appreciate you stepping in. I know you're not an investigator, but—"

"No, I get it. And I have done this sort of thing. All junior prosecutors cut their teeth on research. Give me a day or so. We'll see what I can come up with." He shook her hand, then bade her farewell.

Back in his car, he tossed the photocopies on the passenger seat and started the vehicle. Hand on the shifter, he glanced at the pictures. The lump in his stomach grew and so did his sense that he'd seen those runes somewhere before. He just wished he could remember where.

"James, dinner's ready." Sara glanced through the kitchen doorway to where he sat at the dining table, staring at his laptop screen. He didn't budge. Frowning, she plated two servings of the spaghetti she made, along with a helping of salad, and carried them to the table. "James?" She set a plate on the table to his right, then laid a hand on his shoulder.

He jumped and looked up. "Hey, sorry. I got engrossed in this."

Sara glanced at his screen. Some runic language stared back at her. "What is that?"

"Runes. More specifically, Futhark. It's what was carved into Benny's body."

"Why would someone carve runes into a body?" She set her plate down and sat in the chair next to him.

"I think it might be some kind of ritual. They all have some connection to prosperity and rebirth. Almost like a blessing. What I don't understand, though, is if the killer wanted Benny to have a blessed afterlife, that means he cared, right?"

"Right."

"So, why did he dump his body in a field where the animals and elements could get to it? The early Germanic tribes buried or cremated their dead." He ran a hand through his hair. "It just doesn't make any sense."

She nudged his plate toward him. "Eat. Maybe the fuel will help your brain."

He sighed and closed the laptop lid, then picked up his fork. "Thanks for dinner."

Sara smiled. "You're welcome." She covered his hand with hers for a moment. As she pulled away to eat, her gaze traveled over the copies of crime scene photos, and she blanched.

"Oh, sorry." He scooped them into a loose pile and flipped them over.

She took a drink of his water, having forgotten to get herself a drink. "Thanks." After another sip, she felt her equilibrium return and sent him a curious frown. "Why did Katy ask you to look into all this?" She'd arrived home to find him deep into his research. She'd barely gotten a kiss before he turned his attention back to it.

"I did a lot of research in law school and as a junior prosecutor. I'm also pretty good with languages. She needs another investigator, so I volunteered to help. I just hope this information will help her figure out who did this. I can't help but feel like I'm missing something."

Sara swirled pasta onto her fork. "Like what?"

"Like I've seen this before." He twirled some spaghetti onto his fork and ate it.

"Where?"

"That's the thing. I can't remember. Only a vague recollection of symbols carved into a body. I can't even tell you if they're the same ones."

"Well, pass the information along. She can search whatever database it is she searches for something like that."

He nodded. "I will. I'm going to call her after dinner." He blew out a breath. "But right now, no talk of death. How was your day? I'm sorry I didn't ask when you got home."

She smiled. "It was fine. Busy as usual. Oh! We had a little fun just after lunch. I was at the register ringing up a customer when I heard a shriek outside. I looked out the front window and Marla had her back pressed to the hood of a car trying to fend off three stray dogs that wanted to lick her."

"What?" James grinned. "Why did they want to lick her?"

"She'd spilled something on herself. We've had a problem with some strays hanging around the dumpsters downtown, so all the store owners have been more careful about making sure the lids are closed and that the trash makes it into the bin. It's a bear hazard too. Anyway, they've gotten bolder and are hanging out on the sidewalks sometimes. She walked past them a little while before with her order—a meatball sub. She must have dripped sauce or something on her shirt, because they wanted inside her coat bad." She giggled. "The little one humped her leg while the bigger ones pawed at her jacket and licked her all over."

He laughed. "Was she okay? They didn't hurt her?"

She shook her head. "No, she was fine. I ended up running out and shooing them off. Crazy woman wasn't even grateful. She just huffed and glared at me, then said it was my fault and took off for her store."

"How was it your fault?"

"I guess because I made the sandwich? Or because I own a restaurant that produces enticing smells to humans and animals alike." She shrugged and twirled another forkful of spaghetti. "I did call the sheriff's department to report the strays to their animal control unit, though. They don't need to be accosting people, no matter how funny it is."

Sara did her best to keep James distracted through dinner, but she could tell his mind wanted to spend more time on that case. When they finished eating, Sara cleared the table while he got up to use the restroom. She eyed the closed door, a plan forming. Her attempt at levity at dinner hadn't distracted him for long. She needed something better.

Dumping their plates in the sink, she ran down the hall to the bedroom. On the dresser, she spied her quarry. She grabbed it and ran back to the dining room to set it on top of his laptop, then scurried back to the kitchen before he returned from the bathroom.

Elbow deep in soapsuds, she heard his laughter as he found the toy shark. She glanced over her shoulder, grinning, as he appeared in the doorway holding the plush toy.

"Is this supposed to help me find answers?"

She shrugged. "If you want it to. My goal was to make you smile."

He walked into the kitchen. The room spun as he took her face in his hands and pressed a fierce kiss to her lips. "It worked."

She smiled, biting her bottom lip, then soothing it with her tongue. "How about you call Katy while I finish these dishes, then we have that rematch? See who really owns the title of Shark?"

"Oh, you're on, baby."

His low voice rolled over her senses. A shiver ran down her spine.

He leaned in to feather his mouth over hers. "Don't take too long. And you better bring your A-game."

Twenty-Six

Buzzing brought James out of a deep sleep. He swatted the air near his head, trying to make it stop before he realized it was Sara's alarm clock. She had to get up to open the diner. Groaning, he opened his eyes as her warm, naked weight lifted off his chest to slap at the clock.

"Some days, I wish I owned a pub. Then I wouldn't have to get up so early."

He chuckled, the sound rough with sleep. "Yeah, but then who would make me amazing breakfast food?"

"Mmm... good point." Laughter tinged her voice. She sat up, the covers falling away from her torso, exposing her perfect breasts to his gaze. "Are you tagging along with me this morning, or do you need to write?"

James reached out to skim his palm over her breast. Her eyelids fluttered, and she sucked in a breath. He felt her nipple bead beneath his hand and himself stir beneath the sheets. "I need to stay, but not to write. I promised Katy I'd do my best to run down Billy Jeffries's real name. I might write if I have time. You want to give me some extra inspiration before you go?"

"I gave you plenty last night. Or did you forget?"

"Oh no, I definitely haven't forgotten. I earned that shark fair and square." He grinned at her. They'd played a fierce game of strip poker after he called Katy to report on what he found. It had come down to them both in just their underwear when he ended up with a full house to her three-of-a-kind. He'd taken great delight in watching her stand up and shimmy out of those black lace panties.

She leaned over him, her mouth just inches from his. "I'm going to win it back. You know that, right?"

He stretched his neck to get closer. "Promises, promises." James closed the distance and latched onto her mouth.

Sara moaned and wrapped a hand around his neck. He grasped her hips and pulled her on top of him, thrusting up through the blankets, seeking her sweet heat. She pushed and pulled at the covers to free him while he arched an arm back toward the nightstand, searching for the box of condoms. He found them just as she uncovered him. Her mouth closed around him before he could do anything.

"Sweet Jesus."

She raked her teeth over his shaft and bit down lightly. James's hips left the bed. He growled and flipped them over. She squeaked, then giggled.

"You don't have time for me to recover, so none of that." He ripped the foil packet open with his teeth, then sheathed himself with one hand. Looking up, he saw her pout. "Really? You're disappointed that you get to ride me sooner?"

She giggled again. "Well, yeah. I was looking forward to a little snack before breakfast."

"Hmm... Maybe tomorrow we can set the alarm a little earlier. Then you won't be so rushed."

Sara brushed a lock of his hair away from his forehead and raised her face to his. "Or we could just go to bed early tonight."

"I like the way you think." He scooted forward, forcing her legs wider. Hands under her knees, he opened her up to his view and ran a finger through her wetness.

"James." The word came out on a guttural whisper. He watched her throat work as she swallowed. "This is supposed to be a quickie, remember?"

"Oh yeah." He replaced his finger with his sheathed erection and drove home. They both moaned as he filled her. He paused long enough for her body to adjust to his intrusion, then pumped into her. Her airy moans and his low grunts filled the room alongside the sound of flesh hitting flesh. Her breasts bounced and swayed with the motion of his thrusts, making him harder and driving him faster. Her knees quivered under his hands, and he knew she was close. That was good. So was he.

Shifting his grip on her legs, he tilted her hips. She let out a wild shriek as he hit just the right spot. Wanting to prolong the pleasure just a little while longer, he slowed his pace. She growled and gripped his forearms.

"Don't make the shark bite, Jimmy." She wiggled her hips, trying to make him move faster, but he controlled her legs, so she was at his mercy.

Eyeing the woman lying flushed on the bed in front of him, James had the urge to hold her close as she fell apart. He leaned over her and scooped her into his arms, then sat up with her straddling him. The change in position sent them spiraling toward bliss, and they both broke after just a few strokes.

James held her trembling body close to his as they rode the waves together. Her breath came in short pants close to his ear, sending goosebumps down his spine. He curled his fingers into her hips and ground against her as her body milked every last drop from him. Finally, their orgasms ebbed, and they were able to draw a full breath.

He lifted a hand to smooth her hair away from her face. His fingers caressed her soft cheek, and he touched his lips to hers in a tender kiss. "To be continued."

She bit her lip around a smile and nodded. James helped her slide off of him, then removed the condom, tying it off.

Sara pushed him back onto the bed. "Go back to sleep. You'll need your strength later." She took the condom from him after giving him a languid kiss, then disappeared into the bathroom.

James rested a hand on his chest and stared at the door. He could get used to mornings like this. It had been a long time since he'd awakened to a woman in his arms and hadn't been eager to end their encounter. He never wanted Sara to leave.

But he knew life didn't work that way. They had jobs and responsibilities. There would be time for them later tonight, though. He'd have to think of some twists to card games they could play. Maybe trading favors instead of losing clothes when they lost a hand at poker.

A smile lifted one side of his mouth. Yeah. He liked the idea of that.

Fatigue pulled at his limbs and he drifted while Sara got ready for work. She paused beside the bed long enough to give him another kiss, then disappeared from the room. He heard her moving around in the kitchen, getting coffee before she headed out the door, but was too comfortable to get up.

About an hour after she left, he finally climbed out of bed and took a shower. He'd see what he could find out about Jeffries, then maybe get some writing done before he ran to town to talk to the sheriff about the investigation. See if any of the information he sent last night panned out. Then he'd have lunch with Sara before coming back to get some writing done. He might even stop and get stuff to make dinner tonight. Sara could bring something home with her, but he wanted to make dinner. Take care of her for once.

Plan set, James ate, then sat down at his computer. His Atlanta contact didn't pan out, so he found the local newspaper for Bennettsville and did a search of their online archives, but it only went back twenty years, so he widened his search to the bigger papers. The Atlanta Journal-Constitution had over a century digitized. On a hunch, he ran a search for surviving teenage victims of violent attacks. He doubted he'd get a name, but it might give him something to work with so Katy could request more information from the police department that handled the case.

In a May issue of the paper from twenty-five years ago, he found a mention of a surviving teenage victim of a violent killer. The article went on to state that all the victims had symbols carved into their bodies and that the police didn't know what they meant. The boy who survived had similar wounds and escaped when the man holding him failed to tie him up and he jimmied the lock on the cellar door.

James hit print, and Sara's wireless printer spit out the article. If Billy Jeffries was the boy, he wasn't the killer. He was a victim and could be in danger. Gathering the papers, he donned his coat and boots and ran out to his car.

On his way to town, James went over the case in his head, but came up against a brick wall. With no suspects, he didn't know where to look. He hoped Katy could get something useful from this information. James knew he could have called her with it, but he still wanted to have lunch with Sara and stop at the grocery to get stuff for dinner tonight.

Thoughts of Sara led him to his mental checklist of all the things he needed to do in the next few weeks, including flying home to pack up his apartment, then driving back here with his own car. Though he wasn't sure his little sports car was the best option for Montana. He added trading it in for an SUV or truck to his list. James knew they were moving fast, but he wasn't willing to attempt a long-distance relationship any more than Sara. He'd find an apartment or house in town if she didn't want him living with her yet, but he would not stay in Chicago.

Slowing as he entered Pine Ridge, he drove down the main drag until he saw the sheriff's department. He angled his rented vehicle into a space in front of the building and got out, the article on the murders in hand. Inside, the desk sergeant greeted him and showed him back to Katy's office. The sheriff had the phone wedged between her shoulder and ear as she typed. Spying him, she held up a finger. James leaned against the doorway and waited for her to finish her call.

She hung up and turned to him. "Sorry about that. Have a seat."

James entered the room and sat down, crossing an ankle over his knee. "Did you get anything from the information I sent you last night?"

"Not yet. I've been busy with a burglary case all morning." She glanced at the papers in his hand. "What did you find?"

He passed her the article. "A case in Bennettsville that matches Benny's murder."

She glanced up, surprised. "That's where Jeffries's prints matched to."

"Yeah. I think Billy's the victim mentioned in that article. He's not our killer."

Katy skimmed the papers, her eyebrows winging upward as she read. She laid them down with a puff of air. "Well, shit. We need to find Billy Jeffries."

"If he's even still alive."

The serious set to her jaw said she'd had the same thought. "I'm going to contact their police department and get whatever information I can on this case. Maybe it'll help us figure out who it is. Thanks for the information, James." She lifted the phone from its cradle.

James stood up, recognizing the dismissal. "Yep. Let me know if you need anything else."

"I will." As he left, he heard her ask her administrative assistant to get the number for the Bennettsville, Georgia police department.

Outside, he inhaled a breath of the chilly early December air and glanced at his watch. It was a little early for lunch yet, but he turned toward Sarafina's anyway. Maybe he could get Sara to sit with him for a few minutes and have a cup of coffee.

His long legs ate up the ground as he walked down the sidewalk. He could have driven, but the walk would help clear his head. This was the first time he was on the outside looking in on a case, and it bothered him not to be more involved. As a prosecutor, he'd been able to have a more actionable role in cases. But for this, he was just a consultant. He'd done what Katy asked and fulfilled his role. There was nothing more he could do right now.

The bell on the door sounded as he stepped inside. His stomach rumbled as the smells of fried eggs and sausage met him.

A glance around the room told him Sara was most likely manning the grill in the back. He waved at Rachel, then stepped through the kitchen doors. Sara flipped an omelet on the grill, then picked up an egg to crack it onto the hot surface.

"Hey." He walked up behind her, sliding his hands around her waist to press a kiss to her cheek before stepping back.

She smiled at him over her shoulder. "Hi, you're early."

"Yeah. I found some information online about Jeffries and Benny's murder, so I came in early to talk to Katy."

Sara gave him a curious frown. "Really? Give me a few minutes and I'll be able to take a break. The rush is finally dying. You can tell me about it then. Do you want anything to eat?"

"I think I'll just grab a muffin and some coffee."

She gave a quick nod. "If there are any chocolate chip ones left, get me one, would you?"

"Sure. You want coffee?"

Again, she nodded. James backed through the door and moved behind the counter to get their muffins and coffee. He sat down in a booth by the front windows just as Sara came out of the kitchen. She smiled at her customers as she made her way to him, stopping to talk to a few before she finally slid into the booth.

"I'm hungry," Sara said, reaching for her muffin. "It's been busy and I could use a pick-me-up."

He smiled and peeled the paper off his cranberry orange muffin. "It's always busy."

"True. So, how did your research go?"

"Interesting. Billy's not our killer."

She paused, her muffin halfway to her mouth. "What? How do you figure?"

"He's a victim. I still don't know his real name, but when I was trying to get a lead to get us to it, I found a case in Bennettsville that's similar to Benny's. Teenage boys and young men showing up stabbed to death and carved with ancient writing. One boy got away. I think Billy's that boy."

"Oh my goodness. What did Katy say?"

"She was on the phone to Bennettsville PD to get the case file when I left. Have you seen Billy today?"

She shook her head. "No. I haven't seen him since last Wednesday when he helped me unload my car." She frowned and set her muffin down. "I hope he's okay."

So did James. Now that he knew the reason for the man's odd, gruff demeanor, he wanted to do what he could to make sure he was all right. "Do you know where he lives?"

Sara nodded. "County Road 18. You turn left off the highway up to the Stone Creek, and he's about a mile down. Why?"

"I might drive up there. See if he's around."

"Are you sure that's a good idea? I'm sure Katy's already had a deputy out there at least once."

He shrugged. "Probably. But it doesn't hurt to check again. Maybe he'll come out and talk to me since I'm not a cop."

"He's never had any issues with the law, though, so why wouldn't he come out and talk to Katy or one of her deputies?"

"I'm not sure. But I can't just sit around on this." He'd been the one to point the finger at Jeffries, when all along he was a victim. James needed to make it right and help in any way he could.

Sara studied him over the rim of her coffee cup. "I'm not going to persuade you to stay away, am I?"

Mouth flat, he shook his head. "I'll be careful."

"You better be. We've got a shark to battle over tonight."

Twenty-Seven

Snow crunched beneath James's tires as he turned onto Jeffries's driveway. Small drifts covered the ruts. It didn't look like anyone had been here for days.

He passed through the trees to a clearing. Steam rose from the furnace chimney, but otherwise the place looked deserted. Nothing moved, and no lights shone in the windows.

Getting out of his car, he walked up to the attached garage and looked through the window. Jeffries's ancient pickup sat inside. Maybe he was home. He walked back around front and up the steps to knock on the door. "Billy? It's James O'Malley."

When he got no response, he knocked again, then stepped to the side to look through the front window. Nothing looked out of place and nothing moved. With still no answer, James stepped off the porch and jogged around back. He knocked on the back door, but didn't expect an answer. A glance through the window revealed more of the same as the front. Everything looked fine, but the house appeared empty.

The cluck of chickens drew his attention to the animal pens behind the house. No fresh footprints marred the snow to the barn. He trekked across the yard to the chicken coop. When the hens spotted him, they flocked to the gate, clucking up a storm. James realized they were hungry. It was the same way the chickens on the Stone Creek acted in the mornings when they went out to feed them. Except these birds were much more vocal about their hunger. He wondered how long it had been since they were fed.

A bad feeling settled in the pit of his stomach. Billy wouldn't leave the birds unfed. If he'd run off on his own, he would have either slaughtered them, given them away, or asked someone to feed them. The pens were in too good of shape to indicate any kind of neglect.

James let himself into the run and found the grain bin. The birds flapped their wings and tried to reach the scoop in his hand as he took it from the container. He threw a scoopful of grain over their heads to get them to back off, then filled a bucket and took it to the low trough on the side of the coop. He made sure they had water, then left the run to check on the other animals. A few cows milled in the pasture alongside a horse. He tossed a few cakes of hay into the feeder, which was low, broke up the ice over their water trough, then checked on the goats. They, too, needed food and water.

Once all the animals were taken care of, he went back to his vehicle and called the sheriff.

"Sheriff Lattimer." Katy picked up after several rings, sounding distracted.

"Hey, Katy, it's James. I'm up at Billy Jeffries's place. You said you sent a deputy up here, right?"

"Yes. Why?"

"When was that?"

"Right after we talked Friday."

"I don't think anyone's been here since. None of the animals had food and the water troughs were frozen over. The heat's on in the house, because I can see steam coming from the chimney, but there's no one home."

"He didn't just leave, then." She groaned. "Okay. I'll put out a BOLO on him. Maybe see about getting a judge to sign a warrant for us to go in and do a welfare check. His truck was there when the deputy checked. Is it still?"

"Yes."

"Dammit. All right. Thanks." She hung up.

James turned off the screen and set the phone in the cup holder, then started the car. He glanced over the property once more, but nothing stuck out as unusual. "Where are you, Billy?"

Shaking his head in frustration, he turned around and headed back to Sara's.

His frustration mounted as he ran the case through his head. They had a lot of questions, but not many answers. Billy was the key to it, but it was anyone's guess where he was. James just hoped he wasn't dead.

Back at Sara's house, he did his best to shove the matter out of his mind as he put away the groceries he bought before he left town. There wasn't anything else he could do, and he had a book to write.

He opened the freezer to put away the frozen mixed vegetables he bought for shepherd's pie. His eyes roved the shelves, looking for any little nook where he could put the bag. "Does she even know what half this stuff is?" He sighed and pushed on the frozen bags and containers, trying to shift them and create a modicum of space. A small alcove appeared on the second shelf and he set the bag in it. As he swung the door closed, it tipped forward and smacked the kitchen floor with a rattle.

Sighing and shaking his head, he bent and picked it up, putting it back. He swung the door closed faster, giving a satisfied huff as it shut with the vegetables still inside.

"Hello, Mr. O'Malley."

James jerked and looked to his left. A man stood in the kitchen. "Who the hell are you? How did you get in here?" He backed toward the counter and Sara's knife block.

The man lifted a gun. "Ah-ah-ah. I wouldn't do that."

James froze and stared at the man. "Who are you?" He took stock of the stranger. A black stocking cap covered reddish blonde hair. Hard, pale blue eyes stared back at him from a ruddy face. The man looked a bit familiar, but James couldn't place him.

"Ronan Montgomery."

The man paused, watching him. James frowned. "Is that supposed to mean something to me?"

A cold smile lit the man's face. "No. I just wanted to see how you'd react to the fact that I told you my name."

Comprehension punched James in the gut. Montgomery intended to kill him.

A fierce determination to keep that from happening straightened James's spine. If this guy wanted to kill him, he'd have to fight for it.

A low laugh rumbled from Montgomery's chest. "Well, well, well. You do have balls. I wondered after the stories I heard about you and your sister."

Surprise flickered in James's eyes. "What did you hear?"

"Lots of things. Like how you and your brothers bullied Daisy. How she ran to escape from you. Then how she forgave you all." He scoffed and rolled his eyes. "Pathetic. Both her for forgiving you, and you for letting her leave in the first place. I don't understand why six of you couldn't keep control of one woman. I admit, she seems like a handful. But if she wanted true independence, she'd have stayed gone. Now, you all just look weak."

What a nutball! He talked like he and his brothers should have locked Daisy in a tower and thrown away the key. "How do you know all that?" James knew he probably read it in the tabloids, but he needed to stall while he thought of a way to get the gun.

Montgomery shrugged. "People talk. I listen. Most of them don't notice me. I'm very good at fading into the walls. It's how I've gone under the radar all these years. No one sees me."

The vague recollection of a face at the church hit him. He realized Montgomery was one of the homeless men who'd come in for a meal. Was he really homeless or just pretending to be? "Why the interest in me?"

"No special reason. I paid attention to everyone in town. Especially you and your lady friend after you found that boy's body."

Suspicion narrowed James's eyes. "Did you kill Hunter?"

The first hint of a crack in the man's hard mask showed at the mention of Hunter's name. "That, unfortunately, didn't go as planned. I didn't do enough research on the kid before I snatched him. He was much more—adept—at martial arts than I would have guessed."

James shifted, bringing him closer to the knife block. "Why did you kidnap him? Was it because of his father?"

"Partly. Targeting a cop's kid adds to the thrill, but no, that's not why."

"Then why? I want to understand." His hand edged backward. The knives weren't far now.

Ronan's face closed off. "I'm sure you do. But you'll have to go to your grave wondering. I can tell you that you stuck your nose where it didn't belong. You should have left Rob alone."

James didn't have a chance to do more than wonder who Rob was before Montgomery straightened his arm, preparing to fire. Snatching a knife from the block, James threw it as he fell away, doing his best not to get shot.

The gun firing echoed off the walls. James kept moving, darting out of the kitchen toward the living room and the front door. A bullet slammed into the wall in front of him, and he dove over the couch to safety. Two more ripped through the cushions, embedding themselves in the floor near his head.

"You might as well come out, James. This is a small house. You're trapped in the living room with nowhere to go. How about if you come out now, I'll let you live awhile longer? You can come keep Rob company."

Was Rob Billy? James thought furiously. Giving up right now might be Billy's only chance. But Montgomery could also be bluffing and shoot James the moment he emerged from cover.

Feet appeared around the edge of the couch. James looked up into the barrel of Ronan's weapon. *Fuck! The guy moved quietly.* He hadn't heard him walk around the couch.

The man tilted his head. "I really should kill you now." He lowered his gun. "But there's just no fun in shooting someone. Get up."

James glared at him from his hands and knees. Montgomery raised the gun again.

"Make no mistake, I will shoot you if you don't cooperate."

Gritting his teeth, James got to his feet. "I'm standing. Now what?"

"Now, we take a little trip. Go out the back door."

Eyes sweeping his path for a weapon, James headed for the door. His gaze landed on the knife block, but the gun barrel in his back kept him moving. Maybe once they were in the car and Montgomery's attention was on the road, James could get a message to Katy or Sara. They could get location data from his cellular carrier and track his phone.

The wind bit into James's torso without his coat as they

walked down the driveway to the car parked just out of sight of the house.

"Open the door and get in."

James pulled the handle and lifted a leg into the vehicle. As he shifted to sit, he caught sight of Montgomery's gun hand coming at his head a split second before the butt of the weapon collided with his temple. Pain exploded through his brain, then the world went dark.

Twenty-Eight

"James? I'm home." Sara let herself in through the garage door. She hung her purse on a hook next to James's black parka, then dumped her keys into it with a clink. Taking off her coat, she hung it next to her purse.

"James?" Did he decide to do more research and get lost in it again? He better be working on his novel. She wandered into the living room. Tufts of white stuffing littered the floor near the coffee table. The leather on the back of the couch gaped in two places, showing off the fabric-lined back. "What the hell?" Her gaze bounced around the room. She noted a hole in the plaster near the front door. That looked like a bullet hole.

"James!" She ran down the hallway to the bedroom, but it was empty, just like the living room and kitchen. Quickly looking in the other rooms, she found no sign of him. With trembling hands, she took out her phone and called for help.

"Nine-one-one, what's your emergency?"

"There are bullet holes in my walls and couch and my boyfriend is missing." Saying the words out loud made Sara's stomach roll. She pressed a hand to her abdomen and willed herself not to puke.

"Do you see any signs that someone was injured?"

Sara inhaled a deep breath through her nose and looked around. She didn't see any blood. "No. Other than the bullet holes, nothing is amiss."

"Okay. I have your address here. Can you verify it for me?" The dispatcher rattled off Sara's address.

"Yes, that's correct. Can you make sure the sheriff knows about this? I think it might be connected to Benny Rowe's murder. James was helping her." Sara's voice broke. She swallowed hard to hold back a sob.

"I will, yes. A unit is on the way to your location. No one else is in the house with you, correct?"

"That's right. I searched, looking for James. I'm the only one here."

"Okay. Just stay on the line with me until the sheriff's department gets there. It should only be a few minutes."

Sara returned to the kitchen and sank onto a bar stool. Her eyes landed on another bullet hole in the wall underneath the cabinets. A knife lay on the floor by her feet. At least she knew he fought back. And that he hadn't been shot. Not here, anyway. There was no blood anywhere in the house.

Sirens split the air, and Sara exhaled a sigh of relief. Help was coming. She told the dispatcher she heard sirens, then hung up, going outside to greet the responding deputy.

To her surprise, it was Katy. The tall blonde climbed from her cruiser, a fierce frown on her face.

"What happened?"

"I don't know. I came home and there were bullet holes everywhere and no James. How did you get here so fast?"

Katy's jaw worked. "I was at Billy Jeffries's house, checking things out. James called to tell me it was deserted, and no one was looking after the animals. I was hoping there would be a clue about what happened, but all I saw were some angry chickens. They'd caten all their grain already, so I filled the box again."

Billy's was deserted?

"Show me the damage in the house," Katy said before Sara could wonder more.

Spinning on her heel, Sara led the sheriff inside and pointed out the bullet holes. "What's going on, Katy? James said Billy's connected to Benny's murder, which is connected to a case in Georgia. Now Billy and James are both missing?"

"Yeah." The sheriff rubbed her forehead and blew out a breath. "Twenty-five years ago, there was a serial killer on the loose in Bennettsville, Georgia. He killed four young men between the ages of eighteen and twenty-two in a six-month span. One about every six weeks. A fifth victim, seventeen-year-old Robert David Kline, escaped the killer and reached safety, but not before the man carved runic symbols into his back and chest. Robert David Kline is now William Dane Jeffries."

"What?" Sara breathed. "Oh my God." Her mind spun, landing on one horrifying thought. "Does the killer have James?"

"It's possible, yes. I think he has Billy. Or had him and now Billy's dead, but we haven't found his body yet."

Sara's knees gave out, and she sank onto the arm of the chair in the living room. Her eyes landed on the stuffed shark sitting on the coffee table where they left it last night. Tears welled and spilled over. "How do we find them?" She turned bleak eyes on Katy.

"By following the clues. James was here. His car is still here, which means our killer didn't surprise him anywhere else. He must have followed James, surprised him, then taken him in his own vehicle. Do any of your neighbors have doorbell or security cameras?"

Sara sniffed. "Um, I'm not sure."

"I'll send deputies out and have a look. Is James's phone here?"

"I don't remember seeing it. Do you want me to call it?"

"No. If he has it on him, we don't want to alert the killer to its presence. I'll get an exigent circumstances warrant for his location data. Maybe we'll get lucky." She pulled out her cell and dialed. Placing a hand on Sara's shoulder and giving it a soft squeeze, she walked away.

Sara covered her face with her hands and bit back a sob. She couldn't lose it. It wouldn't help matters any. She needed a clear head and to help in any way she could. And she needed to call Daisy.

Taking out her phone, she dialed Daisy's number.

"Hey, girl. Why are you calling me at this hour? Aren't you home making kissy-face with my brother?"

A watery laugh bubbled out of Sara's mouth. "I wish. Daisy, James—James is missing."

Silence met her words.

"Daisy?"

"What do you mean, he's missing?"

"I mean, I came home to bullet holes—but no blood—and no James."

"Bullet holes! Why would someone want to shoot James?"

"It's complicated. Can you come to my house? I'll explain then. Katy's here and I think she's calling in a team to process the scene. They're going to see if any of my neighbors have security footage. She thinks they left in the suspect's car. This far out of town, it should be easy to spot a strange vehicle."

"Dear God. Okay. We're on our way."

~

Cold seeped through James's sweater into his back. Pain pounded behind his closed eyes, and he could feel something wet on the side of his face and down his neck. Groaning, he lifted his head, opening his eyes. Darkness greeted him, the only light coming from a small lantern behind him. He shifted onto his side and pushed himself into a sitting position.

"I was beginning to wonder if you were ever going to wake up."

James froze at the soft male voice. He turned toward the light. Billy sat on a cot, the light on a crate next to it.

"Billy? You're alive?"

Billy snorted. "Yeah. Wish I wasn't." Even in the dim lighting, James could see the sadness in his gaze. "You'll wish you weren't either soon enough."

James pushed to his feet, shooting a hand out and stumbling into the wall as the room spun. He clutched his head. Dirt crumbled beneath his fingers as he gripped the wall. Firm hands took hold of his shoulders.

"You better sit down." Billy guided him to the cot.

"Thank you." James sank onto the thin mattress, shooting Billy a grateful look.

The bed creaked as the older man sat next to him. "Why are you here?"

Hissing as he probed his head wound, he glanced at Billy. "What do you mean? Our psycho friend brought me here."

"Yes, but why? I know why I'm here. What does he want with you? You aren't his type."

Alarmed, James lowered his hand to face the other man. "His type? Billy, what happened to you twenty-five years ago?"

Billy stood and crossed to the wall, leaning a palm against it for a moment before turning to look at James. "What do you know?"

"That you changed your name. You gave me some creeper vibes with the way you hung around Sara. After we found Hunter Goodman, I suggested to Katy she look into you. Then Benny's body turned up, and she discovered you didn't exist up until twenty-five years ago. We found your prints on a box you helped Sara bring into the church. They matched a sealed file in Bennettsville, Georgia, so I did some digging and found out about the murders. Katy requested the police files, but I don't know what she learned. Aethelred out there grabbed me first." He pointed toward the door set high into the wall. James realized they were in a cellar of some kind. There was no staircase to the doors, nor a ladder.

"He snuck into Sara's house—I still don't know how I didn't hear him—and tried to shoot me. When I fought back, he decided he liked the challenge and took me with him instead. He also told me his name: Ronan Montgomery."

Billy crossed his arms and shook his head, staring at the floor. "I've spent a quarter of a century trying to outrun that man and my memories of him. All it took was a picture in a tabloid to bring him right back to me."

James's eyes widened as understanding dawned. "Asa?"

Billy nodded. "One of the paparazzi following him around caught an image of me in the background. I didn't even know he was there. I was getting into my truck at the feed store at the same time Asa was. I'd have demanded the guy delete the pictures if I knew. I've gotten careless over the years."

"It's been twenty-five years. You don't even look the same, I'm sure."

"Still, I should have been more careful." Billy stared at the floor, kicking it with the toe of his boot.

"What happened?" James asked quietly. "What did he do to you?"

"Awful things." Billy inhaled a shaky breath and sat next to James again. "I was seventeen. One night in May, I was coming home from my girlfriend's house. My car had broken down, so I walked over there. I was headed home when a car pulled up beside me. Before I could even bend down to see the driver, he hit me with a taser. I remember a vague shape standing over me on the road, then the prick of a needle in my arm. After that, nothing." He swallowed hard, and James saw tears gather in the corners of his eyes. "Not until I woke up in a cellar a lot like this one."

"You were bound, right?"

Billy nodded. "Most of the time, yeah. After he—" he paused and rubbed his chest. "After he carved those symbols into me, he left me untied and threw some rags at me. Told me to clean up." His Adam's apple bobbed. "Once I was sure he was gone, I searched the cellar. The cot he had set up was old, so I was able to break off one of the slats. I used it to jimmy the lock and get out." He motioned to the door. "I think that's why this one doesn't have a staircase."

"No, but there's two of us and if one of us boosts the other, we can get that door open. James stood and walked to the door, looking up. "How did he get me down here?"

"Lowered you over the edge and told me to catch. You're heavier than you look, by the way."

James looked up again. He couldn't see any light on the other side. "What have you seen when he opens it?" He glanced back at Billy.

"Sky."

"Do you know where we are?"

He shook his head. "He drugged me. I woke up in here."

Damn. Not knowing where they were wasn't a plus, but they still needed to get out of here. "Boost me up there, would you?"

Billy moved to stand next to James. He crouched and cupped his hands. James stepped into the cradle and Billy lifted, bracing his hands against his chest.

James pushed against the door. It lifted, then caught. It was locked. "Okay, put me down." Billy lowered him and James jumped to the ground. "It's got a padlock holding it in the middle. If we can bust it free, we can get out of here."

"Bust it free with what? All that's in here is the cot, the lantern, a jug of water, and that piss pot he left us." Billy pointed to the five-gallon bucket in the corner.

Frowning, James assessed their prison. He patted his pockets and realized the guy took his wallet and phone. "Did he leave you with anything in your pockets?"

"No."

"The cot's our best bet, then."

"Yeah, but it's not like the one he used the last time. This one is newer. And the rails are aluminum, not steel."

James bent to examine the cot. The poles weren't fused together. They had interlocking pegs. He flipped it on its side and worked a leg loose.

"What are you doing?" Billy crouched next to him.

"I'm going to flatten one end of this and wedge it into the crack up there. They'll make good weapons, too, if he comes back before we can get away."

Billy took another leg off the cot. Both men stood under the door, assessing it.

"You sure about this?" Billy glanced at him.

"We have to try. I know he's probably planning something for you, and I'm not about to let that happen. He takes pleasure in watching people break. I think it's why I'm not dead. I fought back." James set his pole on the ground and stepped on it, trying to flatten it as much as he could so it would fit in the crack. He glanced over at Billy. "Tell me something."

Billy looked up.

"Why were you so interested in Sara? I saw you sitting outside the diner when we came out. You asked all those questions about her."

The older man's head bent, and he focused on flattening the end of his pole as he answered. "I was just looking out for her. No one else seemed to. She stayed late a lot. I just wanted her to be safe." He looked up. "She's a nice lady. Always treats me kindly, even though I'm a gruff S.O.B." He took a deep breath, blowing it out slowly. "I'm glad she has you now. Pine Ridge is safe, but there are weirdos everywhere. Even here."

James snorted. "Obviously." Guilt schooled his face. "Billy, I—" He cleared his throat and tried again. "I think I owe you an apology. When Hunter turned up dead, I pointed the finger at you."

Billy narrowed his eyes as he studied James.

"I didn't like the attention you paid to Sara, and I judged you based on your appearance and, as you said, gruffness. I'm sorry."

Billy drew in a breath and glanced away for a moment. "I guess I can't be too upset. I know you've been captured too, but at least someone's looking for us. For me. If you hadn't looked into my background, I'd just be another one of Montgomery's victims—again. Except dead this time."

"Still, I'm sorry."

Billy waved a hand and stood, assessing his pole. "Don't be. Let's just get the hell out of here."

James rose, some, but not all of his guilt assuaged, and looked up again. "How about you try to wedge the door open? I'm bigger than you, so it makes more sense for me to be on the bottom." He crouched, laying his pole down and linking his fingers.

"Yeah." Billy twirled his pole like a drumstick. "Yeah."

James liked the determined note he heard in the man's voice. Billy wasn't weak, and the man just needed to keep remembering that. James intended to remind him of it every chance he could.

Stepping into James's cupped hands, Billy steadied himself as James stood. Tucking Billy close, he held on as Billy jammed his pole into the crack between the doors. Metal clanked as he pushed against the lock. James's knuckles started to ache, and he felt his grip slipping.

"Gotta set you down, man." James widened his stance and let Billy drop. He shook out his hands. "Did you notice it give at all?"

Billy's expression soured. "No. I think the only way we're popping that latch is to hit it hard."

"Dammit." James speared his fingers into his hair and paced away, his mind racing. If they couldn't bust out, then they needed to be ready when Montgomery returned. They needed a plan.

He looked at Billy, an idea forming. "You ever seen the Thor movies?"

One of Billy's eyebrows winged upward. "You got a plan to rain lightning bolts from the sky?"

"No, but we're going to play 'Get Help.' Only without me chucking you at the guy."

Twenty-Nine

Voices sounded all around her, but Sara paid them little attention. She sat in a dining chair positioned by the window and stared outside as she shredded the tissue in her hands. It was almost midnight. From what Katy had been able to piece together, James had been missing for ten hours. Scenarios for what he was going through played on a reel in Sara's mind, even as she did her best to block them out.

Commotion broke through the voices. Daisy dragged a chair over to sit next to her.

"Hey." Sara spared her a glance. If she looked at Daisy now and saw tears, she'd lose it.

"Hey." Daisy shifted, crossing her legs. "I think I know a bit how Asa and my brothers felt over the summer after my accident. Waiting is the worst."

"Yeah."

"You okay?"

Sara nodded.

Daisy snorted. "Liar."

Sara didn't say anything, just kept staring out the window.

Daisy's hand landed on her arm, but she stayed silent. Sara

appreciated it. She didn't want to talk, but the company was nice.

They sat together like that for several minutes before Sara chanced a glance at her friend. Her eyes were red-rimmed and her cheeks splotchy. She looked as tired as Sara felt.

"This is like a weird movie," Sara muttered.

"How so?" Daisy turned and frowned.

"It reminds me of one of those romantic mystery or suspense novels, except shouldn't it be me who's been kidnapped?" She glanced at her friend. "Why did this guy take James? It looks like he tried to kill him." She motioned to the bullet hole by the front door. "So why isn't he dead?"

"I don't know. But I'm grateful he didn't kill him. At least he has a chance now."

Sara bit her lip and looked out the window again. "I know." Her voice came out as a harsh whisper. The press of tears made her eyeballs ache. She sniffed and blinked, trying to hold them back. One slipped free. "I just want him to come home. I didn't realize how committed I was to this whole relationship thing until I came home to this." She motioned to the damage in the living room. "I went along with the whirlwind of passion and need we were caught up in without really thinking about what it meant. Now, I can't imagine life without him. Of going a day without him calling me Shark or watching him poke his tongue out and bite it as he concentrates on his novel. Of waking up next to him or his smile as he holds out a mug of coffee to me." She swallowed again and closed her eyes, another tear spilling free. "I just want him back."

Heavy footfalls on the porch drew their attention. The front door opened and Katy stepped inside, shadowed by one of her deputies, determination on her face.

"What?" Sara rose slowly. "What did you find?"

"James's phone last pinged on the road to Billy's house."

"Okay. He said he was going to go there."

"Which he did, but what's unusual about it is the time. It was after he came to town."

Sara glanced at Daisy, then back to Katy. "So, what's he doing up there? Did you check Billy's again?"

Katy nodded. "It's still deserted. Your neighbor down near the highway has a game camera mounted on his barn. Seems he's had some issues with some of his chickens disappearing and wanted to see what was taking them. It caught a dark-colored SUV driving past about ten minutes before James's phone pinged on Billy's road. The neighbor didn't recognize the car." She took her phone from her pocket and pulled up an image. "Either of you recognize it?"

"No. It doesn't look familiar." Sara glanced at Daisy, who also shook her head.

"I don't know who it belongs to. Were you able to see the plate?"

"Sort of." Katy's mouth twisted, and she pocketed her phone. "I forwarded it to the tech department. I'm hoping they can zoom in and get me at least a partial. I have deputies combing the area near Billy's house. There aren't many other homes up there."

"Wait," Asa walked up, having heard the last of the conversation. "There's a place about five miles from Billy's that's abandoned. It's up for sale now. I only know because my friend Knox asked me to look into property here that's for sale."

Katy pulled out a notepad. "What's the address?"

Asa opened his email and told her the address.

"Okay. We'll check it out." She nodded to one of her deputies, who took out his phone and walked away, then turned her attention back to them. "Once I learn anything more, I'll let you know." She didn't wait for them to reply. With a soft smile and a nod, she followed her deputy.

Daisy growled. "I can't just sit around and wait. And forget sleeping."

Sara agreed.

"I need to bake." She looked at Sara. "What kind of baking supplies do you have here?"

∼

James's head snapped toward the doors as they rattled overhead. He glanced at Billy, who gave him a nod and laid down on the floor. One door flew open, banging against the ground as it came to a stop. Metal clinked as a ladder came through the opening. A face appeared. "Rob, get up here."

"He can't. Something happened. I think he had a heart attack or something." James injected a note of panic into his voice. With his nerves on high alert, it wasn't hard.

Montgomery leaned in to look around. He saw Billy on the floor, eyes closed. They'd thought about having him lie down on the cot, but James knew one wrong move and it would tip. They'd alternated the legs so it would stand and not look suspicious, but it wasn't stable.

The man disappeared from the opening, only for his feet to reappear a moment later on the top rung of the ladder. His gun followed, pointing at James. "Stay back."

James lifted his hands and moved to the side. Ronan continued down the ladder and stopped next to Billy. He kicked him in the side without warning. James held his breath, but Billy didn't flinch.

"Well, damn." Montgomery crouched and touched two fingers to Billy's neck.

James pounced. He ran forward, lifting Montgomery's gun arm. The weapon went off, a bullet lodging into the dirt wall inches from Billy's head. The other man sat up, punching Montgomery in the face. James landed a series of blows to his armpit, and he dropped the gun. Montgomery twisted, trying to fight James off, but James had several inches and thirty pounds on the man. He got Montgomery on the ground and twisted an arm behind his back.

"Ahh! Let go!"

"Fuck no. Keep squirming. I'll break it."

"James, move."

James looked up at Billy's cold, calm voice. He held Montgomery's gun and had it pointed at the man's head.

"Billy, no. He's subdued. Put the gun down."

"He deserves to die," Billy growled.

"What he deserves is to rot in prison for the rest of his life with the knowledge that he lost. That you won. Again."

"No one would have to know. We could just leave him down here to rot."

"I'm not a murderer, Billy. And neither are you."

Billy adjusted his grip on the gun, tears streaming down his face. "Why did you do it? Tell me that much. Why!" he roared.

James grabbed a handful of Ronan's hair and sat him up, still holding his arm. "I'd like to know that too. Why did you kill those boys back then? And Hunter Goodman. Were there others?"

"I'm not saying anything." Montgomery's eyes darted between them. His chest heaved.

"Really?" James bent his arm a little higher.

Montgomery groaned.

"How about I break your arm, then let Billy shoot you?"

"You—you just said you weren't a murderer."

"Yeah, well, you bludgeoned a teenage kid to death and dumped him like trash. I might be persuaded to change my mind." He pushed harder on Montgomery's arm.

The man winced and cried out. "Okay, okay!"

James backed off slightly.

Montgomery took a deep breath and licked his lips, shaking his head. "Hunter died because he saw me take Rob. I had to stop him from going to the police. He fell when I tackled him. Right onto a feed bin at Rob's place."

Startled by the man's admission, James looked at Billy. "Why was Hunter at your house on Thanksgiving?"

"His girlfriend's birthday was the next day. Everyone around here knows I do woodworking. He asked me to make her a jewelry box. He was there to pick it up."

"Okay, that explains that." He turned back to Montgomery. "But why did you kill those other boys and try to kill Billy? Have there been others?"

Montgomery chuckled. "Of course there have been others. It's been twenty-five years. I've just gotten better about hiding the bodies. Now, there are no bodies."

"What?" Dread filled James.

"I burned them. It's what I should have done all along."

"Why didn't you burn Benny's body? Why dump him on the Stone Creek?"

"I didn't want to draw attention to this place. Not until after I'd killed Rob and was ready to leave. Then I was going to light the whole place up." His mouth turned down. "I buried that ranch hand. Not well enough, though. Something must have dug him up."

James's stomach rolled. That poor kid.

"If you were here for me, why did you kill that ranch hand?" Billy asked.

Montgomery tried to shrug, wincing again as it tweaked the arm James still had bent at an unnatural angle. "When the urge strikes..."

Bile rose in James's throat. He swallowed hard. "Why carve them? What purpose did that serve?"

"It was a blessing. Meant to welcome them into the afterlife."

Billy yanked the collar of his shirt down, exposing thin white scars on his chest. "These are a blessing? You're a sick fuck. They've been nothing but a reminder of pain and terror for twenty-five years. Why? Why did you kill all those boys?"

"They deserved it. You deserved it."

"I don't even know you!"

"Sure you do. You bagged my groceries. I tried to talk to you. To make friends. You snubbed your nose at me. All of them did," he spat. His face relaxed and sorrow took the place of his anger. "All I wanted was a friend. Like Lucas. But none of you were good enough."

"Lucas?" Billy frowned.

James's expression echoed the other man's as Billy looked away, thinking.

"You mean Lucas Bartlett?"

Ronan's face crumpled. "He was my only friend."

Billy's eyes met James's. "He was the first victim."

"You killed your friend?"

Montgomery glanced back at him, tears spilling down his face. "I didn't mean to. But he said he didn't want to be my friend anymore. That I was too weird. Too obsessed with the afterlife. I just tried to stop him from leaving. We fought, and I stabbed him. And then I couldn't stop."

"Did you carve the runes as a way to say you were sorry?" James asked.

Ronan nodded.

"Even though you're not?" James's voice was hard.

Ronan stared at the ground.

James looked up. "Billy, put the gun down. He's going to pay for what he's done."

The other man's hand shook. For a moment, James thought he would ignore him and shoot Montgomery right between the eyes, but he finally flicked the safety on and lowered the weapon.

That was close. James got to his feet, dragging Montgomery with him. "Come on. Time to go." He glanced at Billy. "You go up first. Keep the gun on him. If he runs, then you can shoot him."

A hard glint shone in Billy's eyes. "Gladly." He headed for the ladder and climbed out of the cellar.

James shoved Montgomery toward the ladder. "Go. And remember, he's just itching for a reason to shoot you. Don't give him one. Also," he pulled the pole from under his shirt behind his back, "he's not the only one armed." He let go of the man's arm and prodded him with the pole. "Move."

Hand over hand, Montgomery went up the ladder. At the top, Billy grabbed his arm and stuck the gun in his ribs while James climbed out. He glanced around, noting Montgomery's SUV parked nearby. Perfect. They would just drive back to town. James could take him right to the sheriff's department. He searched Ronan's pockets and found the keys, pushing the button to make sure all the doors were unlocked. As they neared the SUV, red and blue lights bounced off the trees.

Or maybe the sheriff would come to them. Either way, it was over.

Thirty

The echo of her footsteps bounced off the corridor as Sara ran down the hall at the hospital. Asa and Daisy were close on her heels, Daisy's cane adding an extra clack as they went. Katy had called to say they found James and Billy and were taking both men to the hospital to be evaluated.

Sara spotted the cubicle number the nurse told her James was in and flung the door open, throwing back the curtain. James sat on the bed. A stark white bandage shone bright at his temple against his black hair.

"James." The broken whisper barely left her mouth before she took the two strides across the tiny room to get to his side. He reached out and pulled her into his arms.

Sara didn't even try to stop the tears. They flowed freely down her face as she buried it in his neck. She took a deep breath of his scent, reassuring herself he was real, then leaned back to plant a kiss on his lips. He palmed the back of her head, holding her there for a moment before releasing her.

"Are you all right?"

He nodded and wiped a tear from her face. "Just a bump on the head. Maybe a mild concussion, but I'll be okay."

Sara sniffed and stepped back so Daisy could give her brother a hug, then took his hand. She needed the contact.

"How's Billy?" Asa asked.

"Physically, he's fine. But he's going to need some time and some therapy before he's fine mentally. I think the sheriff already took him home. And speaking of, I'm ready to go."

Daisy frowned. "Have you been cleared to leave?"

James echoed her frown. "Well, no, but—"

"Then you're not ready to go."

Groaning, James shot Asa a look.

The other man smiled. "I'll go see about springing you. Hang tight." He disappeared through the curtain.

Sara perched on the bed. "What happened?"

He relayed the story as well as he could from what he remembered. Sara and Daisy listened, their eyes as round as saucers by the time he was done.

"'Get Help?' Really?" Daisy arched an eyebrow.

James grinned and shrugged. "It worked."

"Still, it was quite the risk." Daisy shuddered.

"We didn't have many options. He'd have killed us if we hadn't tried something. I'm just glad he was arrogant enough to put us together."

The curtain swished as Asa stepped inside, followed by a nurse.

"Mr. Mitchell tells me you're eager to leave us, Mr. O'Malley." The petite, red-haired nurse smiled at him.

"Very."

She strode forward with a sheaf of papers and a pen. "Sign these and you're free to go."

James took the pen and scrawled his name where she indicated. She took the top sheet with his signature, then handed him the rest.

"There are instructions there for wound care and a script for antibiotics. Come back if you experience a severe headache or nausea or the wound gets infected. Otherwise, visit your family doctor in ten to fourteen days to get the stitches removed."

"Stitches?" Sara turned to stare at James. "You didn't say anything about stitches."

"I didn't?" He gave her that innocent, boyish smile he broke out anytime he was trying to soothe her anger.

She glared at him, not falling for it.

His eyes shifted to the nurse. "Am I allowed to fly?"

"Yes. Just hydrate and try to get plenty of sleep the night before. It'll help with the headaches."

"Thank you."

She smiled and left.

"Why do you need to fly?" Sara asked. He hadn't mentioned anything about going anywhere.

He squeezed her hand. "Can we talk about it later? I just want to go home and sleep."

"My home or their home?" She pointed at his sister and Asa. Before today, she would have said he meant her house, but if he was planning a trip without discussing it with her first—most likely to Chicago—she wasn't sure anymore.

James frowned. "Yours."

She nodded once, still frowning.

"Well, I guess that's our cue to leave," Daisy said. She pushed her husband toward the door. "Call if you need anything."

Sara nodded.

Sighing, James swung his legs over the bed. He still had his shoes on. "Can we go too?"

"Yeah. You sure you can walk to the car?"

"Yes. I'm a little dizzy, but it's not that bad. Mostly, I'm just exhausted."

Concern for his health overrode her concern about his

travel plans. She hooked an arm around his waist and led him out of the cubicle.

She'd parked close, so they were bundled into her vehicle and on their way home in minutes. The ride there was silent. James leaned his head against the window and kept his eyes closed. His breathing evened out, and she knew he'd fallen asleep. Her heart ached as she thought about what he'd been through. She was thankful it wasn't worse than it was.

Pulling into her garage, she cut the engine and shook him awake. "James. Hey, we're home."

He sucked in a breath and sat up, blinking in the bright lights of the garage. "Oh. I guess I fell asleep."

"Yeah. Come on. Let's get you into bed."

He nodded and climbed out. Inside, they hung up their coats and left their shoes by the door. She followed him down the hall to the bedroom.

"I need a shower, but I don't want to do anything except crash." He eyed the bathroom door.

"I can change the sheets tomorrow. Just go to bed."

"Join me?" He moved to the bed and pulled his sweater and t-shirt over his head.

Sara nodded and slipped out of her sweater. They both stripped down to their underwear, and Sara donned her pajamas. She couldn't sleep in just her panties. James had no problem sleeping in his boxer-briefs or naked, but she woke up either sweating her ass off or freezing if she didn't wear clothes.

She snapped off the bedside lamp as they crawled between the sheets. James wrapped his arms around her and tugged her into his body. He sighed and closed his eyes. Tears pricked hers. She tried to hold them back, but a hiccup broke free.

"Hey." James rolled her over. "Why are you crying? What's wrong? I'm safe."

She sniffed, but it came out as more of a wet snort. Unable to speak, she curled into his chest.

He ran his hands over her back and murmured soothing sounds while she cried.

"Hey, Sara. Shark, tell me what's wrong."

The use of the nickname helped calm her. Whether he was leaving her or not, she knew he cared. Sniffing hard, she pulled back and looked up. "Are you—are you leaving me?"

"Leaving you?" His brows dipped over his eyes. He sat up and turned on the light. Concern shone in their blue depths. "Why would I leave you? I love you."

Sara's lungs stopped working. Her entire body froze as she stared at him while her brain attempted to process the words. He what? "You love me?"

"Yes. Why do you think I'm leaving you?"

She sniffed again and wiped at her face, sitting up. "You asked the nurse if you could fly. The only place you'd need to fly to is home—back to Chicago."

"Right. I do need to go back to Chicago." He cupped the side of her face, his thumb wiping at the wetness on her cheek. "But not to stay. I need to pack up my apartment, trade in my car, and transfer my money to a bank here. So I can move here."

"Move? Here?"

"We talked about this."

"Not really. We agreed long-distance wasn't going to work, but we never actually talked about you really moving here. It was just an idea we threw out there."

"Well, now it's more than an idea. Sara, baby, I don't want to leave. Today—yesterday, whatever the hell day it was—taught me life can be taken in a blink. And I want to be with you every second I can before that blink happens."

"You do?"

"Yes."

"I keep crazy hours."

"So do I; I'm a writer."

"And I'm a workaholic."

"Good thing I can write from anywhere, including your office or a table at the diner."

A smile started to form on her face as he countered her arguments. "I'm better at cards."

He grinned and shook a finger at her. "That one is debatable. I still hold the trophy."

"Hmm. Maybe I let you win."

His smile disappeared, and he frowned. "Wait. Did you?"

She gave him a coy smile and shrugged a shoulder.

"Oh, there's gonna be a rematch real soon." He grabbed her, rolling her beneath him. "But not tonight. Tonight, I'm going to wrap you in my arms and sleep off some of this headache. I'm going to hold you all night and thank God for bringing me back to you." He brushed a loose curl away from her face. "I love you, Sarafina Katsaros. Even when I'm pissed at you or you beat the pants off me—quite literally—at cards, I will still love you."

Warmth flooded Sara's heart. More tears welled in her eyes and spilled over, wetting the hair at her temples. "I love you too. I didn't think I wanted you. Or any man. But you showed me there's more to life—more to living—than what I have. When I thought you were leaving and taking that away—" She paused and shook her head. "I don't want to live without you."

He smiled. "Good, because I'm not going anywhere. You can even come with me to pack up my apartment. Deal?"

She nodded and stretched her neck up to place a soft but potent kiss on his lips. "Deal."

Epilogue

"James! They're here!" Sara dragged the two giant boxes into the house and shut the door as she called to her husband.

He emerged from the spare bedroom, an instruction manual in his hands. "My books?"

She nodded, kneeling beside one box. Plucking at the tape, she tore it off the top and opened the flaps. "I'm so excited. It's like Christmas!"

He laughed and knelt beside her. She removed the paper covering the books and paused, her eyes lighting up.

"These look amazing!" And they did. At the top of the book, the top quarter of a man's face, to include a green eye, took center stage above the title and a cityscape. It was dramatic and eye-catching.

James picked up a book and turned it over in his hands. "They did a great job with the cover. I like it." He opened the book and handed it to her. "Read that."

"What?" She took the book, curious about what he wanted her to read. She'd already read the finished manuscript. It was amazing. She glanced down at the hardcover novel in her hands and realized it was open to the dedication page. Tears welled in her eyes as she read the words.

"To my wife, Sara. Without you, this book would have never been written, and I'd have been destined to plod my way through a normal spy novel. You taught me that sometimes all that's needed is to find our inner shark. I love you." She looked at him with watery eyes after she finished reading it aloud. "I love you too. Thank you."

He pulled her close and kissed her. "I meant every word." He laid a hand on her burgeoning belly. "I never would have tackled such a cold and calculating character if you hadn't given me the idea, then helped me see I just needed to find that predatory side of human nature. I think this is my best book yet. My publisher agrees." He sighed and looked at the box. "Which is why I'm supposed to sign all these and return them to Charlie so she can ship them to my superfans. She said there's another shipment coming next week I need to sign for the bookstores." His mouth twisted. "At least it'll give me a break from that crib."

Sara laughed. "Well, don't take too long. Baby Shark will be here soon."

He chuckled and kissed her again, then sang the first few bars of "Baby Shark."

She smacked his chest. "I still hate that song."

∼

Thank you for reading *Shark!* I hope you loved it! Want to read Jasper and Katy's story? Check out *Katydid* on Amazon: https://books2read.com/u/3LVGR1

If you'd like to read more about James and Sara (and the other characters in this series), join my mailing list. Subscribers get a bonus chapter or scene after every book! You'll also get access to exclusive teasers, giveaways, and the occasional book recommendation, as well as sneak peeks into my world as I create my stories. Scan the QR code below to sign up and get your bonus scene!

Keep reading for a sneak peek at *Katydid*...

Katydid

PINE RIDGE
BOOK 4

Chapter One

A sharp whistle split the air, rising above the sound of hundreds of hooves pounding the muddy earth. A dog's bark joined the mix. The gray-blue and white heeler ran along the rear of the herd, nipping at the cattle when they tried to stray from the pack. Jasper Hendriks glanced over at his boss, Asa Mitchell, to see him gesturing to the left. Looking over, Jasper saw a steer running away from the herd. He spun his big gray gelding, Castle, toward the cow, cutting it off and shepherding it back into the fold. The animal bellowed its displeasure, sending glops of mud flying as he bucked while he ran back to his friends.

Jasper dodged a baseball-sized chunk and trotted back to his spot on the side of the herd. They were moving this group of yearlings to a different pasture that had a smaller pen attached, so the vet could do a herd check tomorrow. But this lot of steers wasn't having any of it today. All they wanted to do was run off and find the little shoots of grass emerging now that the snow had melted and the warmer spring temperatures had prompted plant growth.

Their newest hand, Tommy, opened the gate to the new

pen. Like a finely oiled machine, Jasper, Asa, and the handful of others with them kept the herd together as it funneled into the pen. Asa's dad, Silas, brought up the rear and latched the gate once the last steer went through.

"Whew." Jasper lifted his hat and wiped his sweaty forehead and face on his shoulder. "They were a rowdy bunch."

"For sure." Asa fanned himself with his hat. "I'm ready for a cold beer and some of Daisy's cookies."

"Sign me up." Both of those things sounded wonderful. So did getting out of this damp heat. It was mid-April, but it was steamy today. They'd had quite a bit of rain in the past week and the temperature today was in the lower seventies. It was muggy.

Jasper leaned back and reached into the small saddlebag attached to his saddle and withdrew a bottle of water. Gulping it down, his eyes wandered over the herd. They had a good crop of yearlings this year. All the steers were a nice size and looked healthy.

He turned toward the barn, ready to get off his horse and do something where there was a fan. It might not be beer and cookie time yet, but it was at least time to work on something else.

As they neared the barn, Jasper saw a sheriff's cruiser coming up the drive. "Hey." He called to Asa, then pointed to the car.

Asa's frown matched his. "What's a sheriff's deputy doing here?" He changed direction. "We better go see what this is about." He turned to Silas. "Dad."

Silas glanced over, and Asa tipped his head toward the driveway. Seeing the car, Silas nodded, and the three of them headed for the fence line.

Jasper dismounted and tied Castle's reins to the fence, then hopped over the rail. As his feet landed, he got a better look at the person behind the wheel and noticed it was the sheriff herself, Katy Lattimer.

"It's Katy," Silas said. "Maybe she's here to see Daisy? Or Sofie?"

She changed direction as she saw them walking toward her. The vehicle came to a halt ten yards away with a squeal of its brakes. The engine still running, the tall blonde sheriff emerged, a scowl on her pretty face.

"Don't any of you carry cellphones anymore?"

Jasper, Asa, and Silas shared a look.

"I had to call Daisy to find out where you were. She offered to call you on the radio, but by that point, I had called all of you and was almost here."

"We have them, but they don't always work, or we don't hear them. Why are you here?" Silas asked. "Is everything all right?"

"No. I need Jasper. We got a call about fifteen minutes ago to look for a pair of hikers who went up to Timber Point, but never made it back down."

Instantly on alert, Jasper straightened, his gaze sharpening. "When did they leave?" Jasper asked. He often worked search and rescue when needed in the area. If he wanted, he could run a search and rescue organization, but liked his job on the Stone Creek too much. He was content putting his tracking skills to use when they were needed.

"This morning. And before you ask, no, they didn't just decide to hike longer. One of them is a nurse at Pine Valley Medical. She was supposed to work a split shift with another nurse today, starting at four. She never showed up. That nurse called the woman's husband—who's on the hike with her—then the nurse's sister when she couldn't get ahold of the husband. The sister called us."

Jasper was moving toward her vehicle as she finished talking. He glanced back at Asa and Silas. "Can one of you take care of Castle for me?"

Asa nodded. "Yep. Stay safe."

He nodded and climbed into Katy's cruiser. "Can you swing past my house? I need to get my gear."

"Where is it? It might be faster for me to send a deputy to collect your things. I know for a fact Goodman can pick a lock." She glanced at him as she pulled away from the pasture.

"I live on the ranch." He pointed toward the main house and the cluster of smaller homes beyond it. "In those bungalows."

Bumping over the grass, she steered the SUV onto the lane that ran between the buildings. Jasper directed her to his white, single-story, two-bedroom house with its wraparound front porch. He was opening the car door as she put the vehicle in park.

"Give me five minutes." He glanced over his shoulder to see her nod. Dashing inside, he ran through the kitchen into the laundry room, then out the garage door to the loft storage, where he kept all his search and rescue gear. He grabbed the stepladder off the wall and set it up, scaling it so he could pull down a tub that contained his backpack, helmet, survival gear, a one-person tent, bedroll, and climbing harness. After snatching two bundles of rigging rope from the wall, he went back inside and raided his pantry for high-protein foods and water.

Piling everything on top of the tub, he went outside. Katy saw him coming and got out to open the liftgate. He set the tub in the cargo area and reached up to close the door. "I just need to change my clothes."

She nodded, and he took off for the house again. He knew time was of the essence. He wasn't holding out much hope they would find the couple before nightfall—it was already after five—but the less time they spent in the wilderness after dark, the better. In mid-April, nighttime temperatures hovered around freezing. Tonight would be a little warmer, but forty-five was still cold if you didn't have the right gear.

In his bedroom, he tugged off his boots and stripped out of his jeans and work shirt, leaving on the gray t-shirt underneath. He pulled on a pair of dark khaki cargo pants, then layered a gray thermal shirt over his t-shirt. Topping it off with a zip-up fleece, he shoved his feet in his hiking boots, tying them with swift movements, then grabbed his jacket, hat, and gloves and headed back to the car.

∼

Katy put the car in gear as Jasper buckled his seat belt. Casting a glance at him, she was surprised by the change in his appearance. He looked like a totally different man than the one who went into that house. It wasn't just his clothes, either. His demeanor had changed. Gone was the quick to smile, flirty man she'd gotten to know over the last few months. In his place was someone who reminded her more of her chief deputy, Ray Hughes. It was a rare day when she got him to smile at one of her jokes.

She blew out a breath. That was probably due more to the fact that she took what should have been Ray's job than his lack of a sense of humor. They'd made peace with the decision, but their relationship was strictly professional.

"You okay?"

She jumped. "Yeah." She kept her eyes on the road and blew out another breath.

"You sure? Because you don't look okay."

"I'm fine," she all but growled. "Just a little nervous about the search and rescue operation. I've worked plenty, but I've never been the point person."

"Do you have someone who can help you?"

"Yeah. My chief deputy. He's only run point once or twice in his career, but he helped Sheriff Lyons all the time." She brushed a stray hair away from her face. "Some days, I wonder what the county commissioners were thinking when they appointed me sheriff."

"You didn't have to accept the job if you didn't think you were ready."

"I know. But I was—am—ready. This is one of the few weak spots in my training. I might have been a dog handler in the Army, but I didn't do search and rescue. I was EOD."

"You were in explosive ordinance disposal?"

She glanced over at the note of incredulity in his voice, flattening her lips together as she took in the look of disbelief on his face. "That look right there is also why I took this job. Just because I'm young and pretty doesn't mean I'm not into things that go boom or that I can't be a good cop."

His expression cleared, and he winced. "Sorry. I knew you were military and a K-9 handler, but I guess I didn't think about what that meant. I didn't know you did explosives."

A dark shroud descended over her. "Yeah, well, I don't talk about it much." She preferred not to relive those memories.

"That bad, huh?"

"Yep."

"Forget I said anything."

"Good plan." She huffed and stared out the windshield, watching the road. Memories crowded in—ones she didn't want. She forced her mind onto a song, singing the lyrics in her head. She'd discovered a long time ago it helped refocus her mind and keep the bad stuff away.

The trailhead to Timber Point was only a fifteen-minute drive from the Stone Creek. Jasper pulled up a map on his phone while she drove, for which she was grateful. She didn't want to talk and risk getting onto a sensitive topic again. Her lack of sleep since she took the position as sheriff had brought back her nightmares, so it didn't take much for the memories to surface. She knew she should have dealt with them better years ago, but it had been easier to wall them off and pretend they weren't there.

When the trailhead sign came into view, Katy slowed down and turned right. She wound up the road through the trees until it opened up to the parking lot, which was rapidly filling with first-responders. She parked and they got out. Her eyes traveled over the assembly, landing on Chief Deputy Hughes. "This way." She motioned Jasper to follow and headed over to her deputy.

Hughes had a radio in his hand. Katy heard a male voice on the other end as she approached, but couldn't make out what he said.

"Any news?"

The deputy looked up as she came alongside him. "Sheriff. Jasper. No news yet." He waved the radio. "That was the fire department. They're bringing the SAR gear."

"I brought my stuff too." Jasper gestured to Katy's cruiser. "There any air support coming?"

"I called the state on the way up here. They're sending a chopper, but it'll be another half an hour before they're airborne. I'm not sure how much they'll be able to see, anyway. It's pretty dense up there."

It had been a hot minute since Katy hiked Timber Point, but she remembered the thick pine forest that gave it its name. Hughes was right; the chopper probably wouldn't be of much help. But they had to try.

"I'll gear up," Jasper said. "Once I get a team assembled, I'll head up the trail and see what I can pick up."

"Okay. John Danner and his K-9 unit are on their way, too, and so are the members of the county hasty teams."

"Good. I'm going to grab my gear." Jasper spun and jogged away.

Hughes held the radio out to Katy. "It's all yours, Sheriff."

Katy stared at it for a moment, then shook her head. "Actually, you keep it."

He frowned. "I'm sorry?"

"This is one area where you definitely have more experience than me. More skill. I'll serve this operation better if I go with Jasper." In addition to her EOD skills, she had extensive EMT training and had kept up her certifications. Katy was good under pressure and at managing people, but there were a lot of cogs in a search and rescue operation, and she wasn't as familiar with how they all worked as Hughes was. She knew she could figure it out, but she didn't want her learning curve to impact the rescue. Until she had more experience and training, Hughes was the best person to run point.

"You sure?" He pulled his arm back.

She nodded. "Yes. I'll take a radio and keep it tuned to what you're doing, so I can learn. I trust your judgment. What's the ETA on the fire department with the SAR gear?" She needed at least a helmet and climbing gear if she wanted to join Jasper on the mountain.

"Twenty minutes. They just left the station."

"Okay. Do we know the missing hikers' names?"

Hughes nodded. "Kayla and Derek Peterson."

"How about a map? Did you bring one with you?" She'd been out on patrol when the call came in, and the closest one to Jasper's location. When she couldn't reach him by phone, she'd detoured to get him, while Hughes drove up right away from town. She doubted he beat her to the scene by much.

He nodded. "It's in my cruiser. We can spread it out in the back while we wait for the command station equipment. It's with the fire department." He headed for his car.

Katy followed. He unrolled a topographical map over the cargo area of his SUV, weighing it down with gear from the back.

"We're here." He pointed to a spot. "The trail winds up this way."

"That a map of the area?"

Katy glanced back to see Jasper peering over her shoulder. He had his climbing harness and helmet on now and was attaching a rope to his backpack as he spoke.

"Yeah." Hughes straightened. "We were just looking at the trail."

Jasper leaned in and traced an area with a finger. "I glanced at it on my phone in the car. The chopper will probably confirm it, but I'm betting there was a rock slide here. It's prone to slides, and with all the rain we've had on top of the snowmelt, I wouldn't be surprised at all to discover the trail covered. The question is whether they're stuck on the other side or whether they got caught in it."

Katy prayed they were just trapped on the other side, trying to find another way down. Or that they'd wandered off the trail and were lost. She didn't want to have to deal with more death. Not so soon after the two murders they had late last year.

∽

WANT TO READ THE REST? DOWNLOAD YOUR COPY AT
https://books2read.com/u/3LVGR1

About the Author

Ashley started writing in her teens and never stopped. Her first novel, Smoky Mountain Murder, came out in 2016, and she has since published two more series and has plans for more. When not writing, you can find her with her nose stuck in a book or watching some terrible disaster movie on SyFy. An avid baseball fan, she also enjoys crafting and cooking. She lives in Ohio with her husband, two kids, three cats, and one very wild shepherd mix.

Website: https://ashleyaquinn.com

goodreads.com/ashleyaquinn

amazon.com/Ashley-A-Quinn/e/B07HCT4QST

Also by Ashley A Quinn

The Broken Bow

A Beautiful End

Wildfire

In Plain Sight

Close Quarters

Scorched

Light of Dawn

Pine Ridge

Sweetness

Loner

Shark

Katydid

Homespun

Foggy Mountain Intrigue

Smoky Mountain Murder

Smoky Mountain Baby

Smoky Mountain Stalker

Smoky Mountain Doctor

Smoky Mountain K-9

Smoky Mountain Judge

Prequel to Wagner Brigade

Stranded with Ezra

Wagner Brigade

Ford's Fight

Dean's Dilemma

Jordan's Journey

Sam's Salvation

Asher's Assignment

Printed in Great Britain
by Amazon